THE ADVENTURES OF SUPERMAN

Jor-el placed his infant son into the model
of the Space Ship. (Page 17)

SUPERMAN

BY GEORGE LOWTHER
Based on the cartoon character created by
JERRY SIEGEL and JOE SHUSTER
Illustrations by JOE SHUSTER
Foreword by JOSETTE FRANK
Staff Advisor, Children's Book Committee, Child Study
Association of America
Introduction by ROGER STERN
Author of the bestseller, *The Death and Life of Superman*

APPLEWOOD BOOKS • BEDFORD, MASS.

TO KEVIN

ISBN: 1-55709-228-1

This is an Applewood Book.
Applewood reprints America's lively classics — books
from the past that are still of interest to modern readers.
For a free copy of our current catalog, write to:
Applewood Books, 18 North Road, Bedford, MA 01730.

Library of Congress Cataloging-in-Publication Data
Lowther, George Francis, 1913
    Superman / by George Lowther; based on the cartoon
character created by Jerry Siegel and Joe Shuster; illustrations by Joe Shuster; foreword by Josette Frank; introduction
by Roger Stern.
        p.   cm.
        Reprint. Originally published 1942.
        Summary: Once he becomes aware of his super powers,
Clark Kent uses them to fight the forces of evil.
        ISBN 1-55709-228-1
        [1. Adventure and adventurers—Fiction.   2. Heroes—
Fiction.]
    I. Siegel, Jerry.   II. Shuster, Joe.   III. Title.
    PZ7. L9675Suc   1995   94-43029
                                                CIP
                                                AC

CONTENTS

ILLUSTRATIONS

vii

FOREWORD

AMERICA has had many fabulous heroes. As our country grew, there sprang up tall tales of men whose wondrous deeds and strength were beyond ordinary men. In the great lumber country men told of Paul Bunyan, mighty logger, who moved mountains and changed the course of rivers to suit the lumbermen. The opening of the West created Pecos Bill, who could lasso a tornado and mount a demon stallion. As the railroads pushed south and west came black John Henry, steel-driver, spitting hot rivets and laying his rails just ahead of the speeding trains. And now—Superman—wrestling with the mechanized might of today's world of airplanes and submarines and super-villainy.

Superman! Most of you who will read this book already know him. Perhaps you have followed his adventures in the comics where first he was introduced to an astonished world. You may have heard his challenging voice on the air-waves of the radio or watched his flaming red cape as he streaked across the screen at the movies. His fame has spread to the four corners of the earth. In South America, in China, in South Africa his broad shoulders and flying cape are a familiar symbol. His exploits are told in many tongues.

Millions of boys and girls in America have acclaimed Superman, strong and invincible, nemesis of evil-doers. Many who have followed his adventures with breathless interest have wondered about him: Where did he come from? Whence came his super-strength and mar-velous powers? They have asked to be told again the story of his origin—of his arrival on earth from a distant planet, of his boyhood and youth, of his first discovery of his super-powers, and of his dedication to the fight against the forces of evil. So here is his story, from the beginning.

JOSETTE FRANK
Staff Advisor, Children's Book Committee
Child Study Association of America
1942

INTRODUCTION

W HAT YOU HOLD in your hands is a little piece of history.

But then, you knew that already, didn't you? After all, this book deals with Superman, and the Man of Steel has been making history for over half a century.

Created by writer Jerry Siegel and artist Joe Shuster, Superman was the first *bona fide* star to emerge from the world of comic books. Introduced in 1938, in the first issue of *Action Comics*, this strange visitor from another planet proved so popular that within a year he had acquired a second comic book entitled simply *Superman*. Within that year, the Man of Steel also began conquering every other medium he could find.

On January 16, 1939, Siegel's and Shuster's new *Superman* newspaper comic strip made its debut. Though the strip began in just four newspapers, within two years more than three hundred papers carried the Man of Steel's adventures, reaching a combined readership of some 20 million.

On February 12, 1940, "The Adventures of Superman" radio program premiered on the Mutual Network. The series became a classic of the Golden Age of Radio and aired throughout the decade.

In September of 1941, the first of seventeen fully-animated cartoons appeared in theaters. Produced by Fleischer Studios—home to Koko the Clown, Betty Boop, and Popeye the Sailor— the Superman cartoons were a milestone in the history of animation and continue to influence the industry today.

And in 1942, the story that you are about to read was first published.

Amazing, isn't it? In just four short years, Superman had become a force to be reckoned with not only in the comics, but on radio, at the movies, and on the printed page. Further success lay ahead for the Man of Steel . . . in motion pictures, on television, and even on the Broadway stage! And from the base of Superman's continuing success in comics, one can only speculate about what cyber-worlds he will conquer in the years to come.

But our purpose here is not to contemplate Superman's possible futures . . . it is, rather, to consider an almost-forgotten chapter of his equally intriguing past.

For, you see, with the exception of a rare — and unauthorized — softcover facsimile copy produced in 1979, this book has been out of print for over fifty years!

This early prose version of the Superman legend was the work of George F. Lowther, who in the early 1940s worked primarily as a scriptwriter for the aforementioned Mutual Radio Network. Born in 1913, Lowther had begun his career in broadcasting at the ripe old age of thirteen, quitting school to become a page for the National Broadcasting Company. In the years that followed, he became a writer of some renown, writing scripts for such long-running comics-to-radio series as "Dick Tracy," "Terry and the Pirates," and—of course—"The Adventures of Superman."

Lowther later added producer's and director's duties to his list of radio credits, and in 1945 made the jump to television with the fledgling DuMont network. In time he would become involved with such classic dramatic anthologies as the "U.S. Steel Hour" and "Armstrong Circle Theater."

In 1963, Lowther lent his writing talents to Westport, Connecticut's Famous Writers School as a supervisor of instructors, but he always kept a hand in the creative end of writing. In the early 1970s, Lowther helped launch the "CBS Radio Mystery Theater." He had contributed over thirty scripts to the series before his death in 1975.

George Lowther was in his late twenties when he wrote *The Adventures of Superman,* a book that was most certainly produced with the juvenile market in mind (although a special Armed Services Edition was also issued that same year for distribution to American servicemen . . . not at all surprising, given the Man of Steel's immense popularity with soldiers and sailors). The fast-paced story not only tells the origin of Superman, but spins a yarn full of haunted shipyards, secret agents, and Nazi saboteurs. In dealing with the latter, Lowther quite pulpishly reflects the paranoia then prevalent in a United States that had just become an active player in the Second World War. Frankly, there are some lapses in the logic of the plot which may seem glaring to the eyes of the modern reader. Still, considering that it was written over fifty years ago—for an audience chiefly composed of boys and young men—the tale holds up remarkably well.

Holding up *extremely* well are the ten full-page illustrations, four of them in color, and the numerous sketches of Superman produced by Joe Shuster and his studio. Shuster, the Man of Steel's premier artist and co-creator, had early on been forced to hire assistants to meet the ever-growing demand for more Superman material. Hurriedly sketching layouts for the stories in pencil, he would rough in the main figures before passing the art boards along to his staff, who would tighten up the pencil drawings before inking the backgrounds and some of the figures. The master himself would then meticulously ink the final renderings of the primary characters. In later years, Shuster proudly recalled that, during the Man of Steel's first decade, he had inked virtually every face of Superman that had appeared in the comics. The power and dynamics of Joe Shuster's Superman are evident in every drawing in this book.

There are many firsts associated with this book. With its publication, Superman became the first comic-book character to have an original adventure told as a prose novel. Also, George Lowther became the first writer other than Jerry Siegel to receive a credit for writing Superman.

And then, there is the matter of Superman's Kryptonian parents. Siegel and Shuster originally presented the alien couple as *Jor-L* and *Lora* in the newspaper comic strip (the two Kryptonians would not be formally introduced in the comic *books* until *Superman* #53 went on sale in 1948). In Lowther's story, for the first time they become Jor-el and Lara. The spelling of Lara would carry over into the comics, and the Man of Steel's sire would eventually become known as Jor-<u>El</u>.

At the time this book was originally written, life on the late planet Krypton had been shown in just ten early installments of the daily comic strip (and not at all in the comic books). It fell to Lowther to flesh out the world of Superman's ancestors. To that end, he introduced Ro-zan, the supreme leader of Krypton's ruling Council, and played heavily upon Jor-el's frustration at being unable to convince his countrymen of their world's impending doom.

More important, within these pages is the first extensive depiction of Superman's early life as Clark Kent and of the couple who raised him. Siegel and Shuster had shown the Kents in just three panels on the first page of *Superman* #1, and had them dead and buried by page two. (The earlier story in *Action Comics* had given the impression that Clark had been raised in an orphanage, as had the newspaper strip. And amazingly, the first radio program had Superman emerging fully grown from the rocket which had borne him to

Earth.) It was not until George Lowther put words to paper that we truly met Clark's parents . . . Sarah and Eben Kent.

Believe it or not, it wasn't until 1952, some ten years after this book was written, that both *Martha* and *Jonathan Kent* became the names firmly recognized within the Superman canon. In *Superman* #1, Pa Kent was not named at all and Ma Kent was only fleetingly referred to as *Mary*! It was not until the aforementioned *Superman* #53 that we would see the names of both—and then only inscribed on gravestones—as John and Mary. In fact, barely a year later, Clark's earthly father is referred to in a story as *Silas* Kent.

That being the case, we can't really blame Lowther for inventing Sarah and Eben. After all, in the matter of the Kent family, he didn't have much source material to draw upon.

At any rate, it was the Lowther version of the story—including Ro-zan, Sarah, and Eben—that was eventually used as the basis of the origin sequences in both opening chapter of Columbia Pictures' 1948 "Superman" serial and in the initial episode of the long-running syndicated "Adventures of Superman" television series starring George Reeves.

There's one last interesting facet to Lowther's novel.

In coming up with a realistic explanation for how the Kents, a normal human couple, could conceivably raise their alien foundling, Lowther chose to discount the two brief scenes from the comics of the infant boy performing amazing feats of strength. Instead, he hit upon the idea of having young Clark's powers manifest themselves gradually. Some four decades later, writer/artist John Byrne—working without the benefit of Lowther's long-out-of-print text—arrived at the same solution for the 1986 *Man of Steel* miniseries which renewed and reestablished the hero in the world of comics. And so, this book has parallels to even the newest version of the Superman comic books.

There have been many versions of the Man of Steel over the years, just as there have been many and differing versions of Tarzan, of Sherlock

Holmes, of Mickey Mouse. That is probably inevitable when a fictional character becomes a cultural icon. But for all the differences in time and place—in names and details—from the hero we know today, George Lowther's Superman still evokes the ideal of Siegel's and Shuster's Superman. And you can't ask for more than that.

— ROGER STERN
September 26, 1994

A veteran comic-book writer—including seven years on Superman *and* Action Comics—*Roger Stern wrote the best-selling novel* The Death and Life of Superman.

CHAPTER I

WARNING OF DOOM

THE GREAT HALL of Krypton's magnificent Temple of Wisdom was a blaze of light. Countless chandeliers of purest crystal reflected the myriad lights into a dome of glass where they were shattered into a million fragments and fell dazzling over the Great Hall.

Below the brilliant dome the Council of One Hundred waited. Attired in togas of scarlet and blue, they looked impatiently for the arrival of

Jor-el, Krypton's celebrated scientist. They had been summoned from the length and breadth of the planet to hear a message Jor-el would deliver. What the message was they did not know. They knew only that when Jor-el spoke all men listened.

Now they waited, curious as to the nature of Jor-el's message. Rarely did the brilliant young scientist leave the mysterious regions of his laboratory. Whatever he had to say tonight they knew would be of great importance to Krypton and its people.

There was a sudden movement and a murmuring wave of voices rose and fell, echoing in the Great Hall.

Jor-el had arrived at last.

All eyes centered on the tall, thin figure that moved forward on the raised platform and took the hand of white-bearded Ro-zan, supreme leader of the Council. There were those who noticed at once that the handsome face of Jor-el was drawn and haggard. Something, they knew, was wrong. The Council of One Hundred waited in hushed suspense.

Wearily, the young scientist turned to the gathering. Standing tall in the yellow and purple robes of his calling, he drew a deep breath. There was a moment's pause and then his voice filled the vast Hall.

"Krypton is doomed!"

Had a thunderbolt crashed through the crystal dome of the Temple at that moment it could not have produced a more startling effect!

Ro-zan rapped heavily for order, and in time the tumult aroused by Jor-el's startling words died down. Silence reigned as the two men, one the aged supreme leader of the Council, the other Krypton's foremost scientist, faced each other. Ro-zan's kindly face was grim as he strove to keep his voice steady.

"Say on, Jor-el."

Jor-el nodded and again faced his audience. He spoke slowly now, carefully, choosing his words.

"Members of the Council, I repeat—Krypton is doomed!"

A gathering wave of protest began, but Jor-el stilled it with a lifted hand. The wide yellow sleeve of the gown he wore fell away from his upraised arm and showed the gauntness of it, accentuating the thin boniness of his fingers. Whether the Councilmen believed him or not, they could see that long hard weeks of toil had aged this man. They listened respectfully as he went on.

"Would that I could bring you good news, but I cannot. Week upon week, pausing for little sleep and less food, I have worked in my laboratory, striving to understand the signs which have come to us from outer space. You, my friends, for months past have seen the sudden showers of stars that have fallen upon our planet. Comets of great magnitude have appeared from nowhere, whirling dangerously close to Krypton. Not many weeks ago a monstrous tidal wave rose from the sea and roared toward our city. Good fortune was with us, for the wave died before it reached our shores. It was then I first realized there might be something wrong and I set myself to discover the meaning of these phenomena. I have found out. Krypton is doomed to destruction."

Again a murmur of protest rose among the Councilmen and again Ro-zan was forced to rap for order. When quiet had been restored, he said, "Jor-el, how explain you this?"

The young scientist shook his head.

"Would that I might answer you, Ro-zan, but even the learned men of science who work under me cannot fully comprehend my equations and formulae. I will be as clear as I can. The Planet Krypton may be likened to a volcano—a volcano that for years has slumbered peacefully. Now it begins to come awake. Soon it will erupt! Whether that eruption will be slow or sudden, I cannot tell. *But it will come!* And when it does, the mighty Planet Krypton will burst into a million molten fragments!"

The glowing eyes set deep in the haggard face of the young scientist held everyone in the Chamber spellbound as he added, "Time is short! I bid you prepare!"

The spell, however, lasted only for a moment. Then, with a mighty surge, a roar of anger and protest burst forth. Jor-el had lost his mind, some cried; others that he had made a mistake in his calculations. He was over-wearied with too much work and needed rest. In brief, they could not and would not believe him.

His arms half-raised, the scientist turned beseechingly toward Ro-zan, a tragic, almost helpless figure.

"Make them understand," he pleaded. "You, Ro-zan, can make them believe!"

Ro-zan's smile was filled with pity. He spoke in a kindly voice.

"Come, Jor-el," he said softly, "surely you have made a mistake. Surely—"

"I have made no mistake! Ro-zan, you must believe—"

Ro-zan's upraised hand commanded silence.

"I understand well what faith you must have in your deductions, Jor-el. But certainly it is difficult to believe the thing you tell us. Krypton doomed? Krypton fated to destruction? Impossible! You yourself must realize that, Jor-el, in your—er—saner moments."

The scientist stiffened, as if Ro-zan had struck him across the face. He waited a moment to master himself before replying. "You think me out of my mind?"

Ro-zan shook his head slowly, smiling patiently as he did so.

"No, Jor-el. I think that not at all. A mind as lordly as yours knows not destruction. But certain it is, friend, that you are weary. You have toiled long and well in the service of the people of Krypton, and you need rest."

"I tell you—" Jor-el began, but again Ro-zan stayed him with an upraised hand. There was now a slight trace of annoyance in the older man's voice.

"Please, Jor-el, this is unlike you! What if your strange deductions are correct? What if your scientific equations and astronomical formulae are true? What can we do about it? Where can we go?"

With desperate eagerness Jor-el seized the opportunity to answer Ro-zan's question.

"I have not come here with this tragic news," he said hastily, "without bringing with me a solution for it. You ask me where we can go? My answer is—to the Planet Earth!"

There was a pause before the Councilmen realized what Jor-el had said. Then the Great Hall rocked with laughter.

"Listen to me! Listen to me!" Jor-el cried over and over again. But his voice was drowned in the thunderous laughter. Even Ro-zan did not rap for order this time, but turned away to hide the sudden smile that came to his lips. Only when the laughter had worn itself out did he again address Jor-el.

"Dear friend," he said, "you see how right we are? You see how badly you do need rest? No —please—speak not till I have finished. You say if Krypton is destroyed we can escape to the Planet Earth. How could we live there, Jor-el? You yourself—you who have studied the Earth for years through the great telescope—have told us how inferior to ourselves are the Earth People. They are thousands of years behind us in everything, mental and physical. Their cities are as nothing compared to the cities that have existed here on Krypton for centuries. Their minds are so far beneath the capacity of our own that actually, in comparison, they have no intellect at all! As for their bodies, you yourself have said that they are weaklings. It takes a hundred Earth People together to do what one man on Krypton can do alone! They have not the power to fly, but must walk at snail's pace on the Earth's surface! They cannot breathe beneath the sea!"

Ro-zan shook his head slowly from side to side.

"Would you send us to live among such a people, Jor-el? Nay, I think not! Death is preferable to life in a world of such inferior people."

"I have studied the problem with the utmost care, Ro-zan," Jor-el persisted. "The atmosphere that surrounds the Earth is the only one that can sustain us. There is no other planet to which we can go, no other—"

"Stop!"

Ro-zan's voice was harsh and his face had become stern.

"I would not be angry with you, Jor-el, but you drive me beyond patience. The Council of One Hundred and I have heard enough. What you tell us is sheer nonsense. Krypton is not doomed, nor will it ever be! You are weary and need rest—I hope it is no more than that. Now, until you have recovered your senses, please come to us no more."

Again Jor-el stiffened, for again it was as if Ro-zan had struck him. After a moment's pause he turned to go, then stopped and faced the Council.

"I will go," he said, bitterly, "but before I do, I would have you know one thing." He paused, letting his eyes rove over the assembly. "I am right. I know this. You must learn it. When you do learn it, I trust it will not be too late. I am at work on a model of a Space Ship——" A titter ran through the audience, but Jor-el did not stop. "——a Space Ship that I had hoped would carry us all to the Earth! I shall continue with my work, for only in that way may I still save you from yourselves when this tragedy comes upon us. And now—I leave you."

Not a word was spoken as Jor-el turned and moved slowly out of sight through the high arched doorway—a tragic, beaten figure.

CHAPTER II

THE SPACE SHIP

A LONG SILVER ROCKET—the model of Jor-el's
Space Ship—gleamed under the powerful
lights of the scientist's laboratory, amidst a clut-
ter of scientific instruments. Jor-el, the sleeves
of his robe rolled back, worked over the model
with feverish haste. So deep was his concentra-
tion that he did not hear a panel in one of the
walls slide back, and did not see his wife, Lara,
as she entered with their child in her arms. She
waited until Jor-el looked up and noticed her.

13

"I heard you at work," she said. "I knew you had returned. What did the Council say?"

Jor-el shook his head sadly. "As you warned me, Lara, they refused to believe me."

"But you intend to continue your work on the Space Ship?"

Jor-el fitted a valve into place before he answered. "Of course! Whatever they think, Lara, I am right—I know it! And if there is still time, I will save them!" He gave the valve a final twist. "I shall start constructing the Space Ship itself as soon as this model is finished."

Lara nodded, understanding. The child in her arms whimpered and she began to rock it back and forth. "Little Kal-el has been strangely restless these past few days," she said. "He has scarcely slept at all. Jor-el, do you think he feels the approach of this thing you have foretold?"

"It may be," said Jor-el. "He has always been sensitive to the elements."

The scientist continued his work, his thin hands moving swiftly and surely over the intricate mechanism of the model Space Ship. Lara sat and watched, rocking the child in her arms.

Finally she gave voice to the question that troubled her. "Is there much time, Jor-el?"

"No," he answered, "there is little time. That is why I hasten to finish the model. It is almost ready. I have only to install the Atomic Pressure Valve and ——"

Whatever he was about to say froze in his throat as an ear-shattering crash burst over Krypton! He clutched the model Space Ship to steady himself, for the entire room was rocking. Things were falling and splintering all about. A tall cabinet filled with tubes and measuring glasses fell with a mighty crash. Gaping cracks appeared in the walls and the cement floor surged underfoot like an awakening monster. The high arched window broke into a thousand fragments. And through the yawning hole where the window had stood, Jor-el saw a seething fan of flame spread upward and envelop the sky.

"It has come, Lara!" he cried. "It has come!"

And come it had! In seconds, night was turned into flaming day. Across the sky, countless comets whirled screaming through brilliant space. The stars began to fall, showering upon

Krypton a rain of liquid fire. Asteroids of every color careened across the heavens. Lights of every size and hue, dazzling and eye-searing, scattered over Krypton.

The elements, as Jor-el had predicted, had gone mad!

Jor-el, a man of science, remained calm in the face of this sudden cataclysm. As the sky fell, as the ground seethed, his mind teemed with the possibilities of the moment. The Space Ship was not ready. It was too late to save the people of Krypton. Too late to save Lara and himself. But the child ——

"Lara!" his voice commanded. "We can do naught for ourselves or the others. But there is hope for Kal-el!"

"Jor-el ——?"

He answered her question before she asked it.

"The model of the Space Ship!" he cried. "I have only to install the Atomic Pressure Valve. A few moments will do it! And then, Lara, if it works ——"

Even as he spoke he was collecting the tools he would need. And as he worked, Lara stood with the child in her arms, gazing out at a crumbling world.

Flames of every color roared from great fissures in the land. Against the frightful glow could be seen the majestic spires of Krypton shattering into dust. And under all this was a strange rumbling, as if some mighty force were stirring fitfully and gathering its strength for one great and final upheaval. Lara knew that when that upheaval came it would be the end.

"It is ready!"

She turned at Jor-el's words to see him standing beside the gleaming silver model.

"Give me the child," he said, "and pray the model works! For in it we shall send him to the Earth and to safety!"

Lara said not a word but placed the tiny form of Kal-el in his father's arms. She watched silently as Jor-el placed it, whimpering, into the model of the Space Ship and closed the steel door. When he was certain the door was sealed securely, he quickly threw a lever.

Together they waited. And, waiting, they heard the strange rumble gathering under them

for the final upheaving surge that would spell
the end of Krypton. As the rumbling increased,
the flaming sky grew brighter, the comets whirled faster, the stars fell in greater showers!

They heard but saw none of this, for their eyes
were fixed on the needle of the gauge that marked the atomic pressure of the model. Something
seemed to be wrong. The needle had not moved.
The pressure necessary to send the steel bullet
hurtling into space was not increasing. But the
ominous rumble beneath *was* increasing, build-
ing toward that final cataclysm that would burst
the Planet Krypton!

Jor-el clutched at the lever, working it back
and forth. He stared at Lara with wild eyes, and
beads of sweat stood out on his forehead. Seconds, literally, stood between the infant Kal-el
and safety. The moment of Doom had come! A
monstrous crash in the distance marked the end
of Krypton! The fissures in the ground opened
into yawning chasms. The laboratory began to
fall about them! And the atomic pressure of the
tiny, futile Space Ship——

The needle moved. There was a hissing, as of

some tremendous skyrocket. Jor-el had only time to let go the lever as the model strained and trembled and, rending loose, shrieked into flaming space, bearing toward Earth its tiny passenger.

CHAPTER III

YOUNG CLARK KENT

E BEN KENT reined his horse to a stop, leaned on the worn handle of his plow, and looked off across the rolling land he had just tilled, to the point where hill met sky. There was something strange about that sky. He knew the weather, as well as any farmer born to the soil, and off-hand he would have said a storm was brewing. Yet he was not quite sure. It seemed to him there was the feeling of something more than just a storm in the air. He had seen that same slate sky before, had felt the same heaviness in the air, had seen the thunderheads rising in the west. And yet——

Eben reflected for a moment, shook his head in a puzzled way, clucked to the horse, and set about finishing the South Forty before night closed in.

He heard thunder rumble in the distance, and thought vaguely that there was something peculiar even about that. Unlike the thunder he had ever heard before, it did not die away but was continuous, increasing in volume. He clucked again to the horse, for the animal had stopped in its tracks with the first rumbling sound, its ears flattened against its head.

As Eben continued his plowing, the sun broke through the heavy slate sky. At least he thought it was the sun, for there was a sudden blaze of light in the heavens, a light that grew larger as he watched it. In the next instant he became alive to the fact that it was not the sun!

The plow was wrenched from his strong hands as the horse reared, screamed in fright, and bolted across the fields, dragging the plow after it. As Eben stood in mute amazement at the animal's singular behavior, he heard a strange whine in the air, and then a distant roar that changed to a series of thunderous explosions. Dizziness overcame the old farmer as the whining filled his ears. He almost cried out for help as, reaching out with his hands, he sought to steady himself. It was then, as he stood tottering and afraid, that the growing blaze he had thought to be the sun struck the earth not far from him. Blinded and afraid, he threw himself to the ground, burying his face in the new-turned loam, his fingers clutching the good brown earth for safety. Then, trying feebly to crawl away on his hands and knees, he fainted.

The crackling of flames was the first sound he heard as consciousness returned to him. The air was unbearably hot, but not so hot that he could not stand it. The thunderous explosions had stopped and the strange whine in the air had

died away. Eben raised his head and looked
about him.

Not a hundred yards away was a strange, bul-
let-shaped object, almost completely enveloped
in flames. Hesitating only a moment, Eben ran
toward it, a conviction growing within him that
someone might be inside that flaming silver
shell.

Peering through the flames, he saw a child lying helpless behind the thick glass window of
the door that sealed the rocket. Already Eben
had come as close as the wall of heat would let
him. He realized instantly that unless he broke
through that searing wall the child would die.

He made up his mind quickly, took a deep
breath, and plunged through to the rocket.
When he emerged again from the flame and
smoke, agony stood in his eyes, for he had been
severely burned. But in his blackened arms he
held the child!

Eben Kent and his wife, Sarah, never knew
where the child had come from, never pierced

the mystery that surrounded his strange appearance on earth. Destiny perhaps played a part in directing the rocket to the Kent farm, for the Kents were childless and desired a child above anything else on earth. And here, like a gift from Heaven, was the infant Kal-el. The old couple took him into their home and raised him as their own.

They called him Clark, because that was Sarah Kent's family name. The circumstances surrounding his peculiar arrival were almost forgotten as year ran into year and the infant grew to be a strong and handsome boy, helping Eben with the chores about the farm, listening to stories at Sarah's knee in the long winter evenings. He seemed no different from other boys of his age. He attended the little country school, played games, went fishing in the hot summer afternoons, and worked and studied as all boys do.

It was not until his thirteenth year that the incident occurred that was to set him apart from ordinary humans, and was to give him his first glimpse of the powers he possessed, beyond those of the earth people who were his companions.

It happened on the last day of school. The pupils of the eighth grade, young Clark's class, waited with great expectations for the arrival of Mr. Jellicoe, the principal. It was Mr. Jellicoe's custom to award personally any prizes that had been won by the pupils during the year—prizes for excellence in composition, mathematics, spelling and so on.

Miss Lang, Clark's teacher, had taken the prizes from the drawer of her desk and placed them on a small table, where the children's eyes could feast on them while waiting for Mr. Jellicoe. There were books of all descriptions, medals, and ribbons. Hearts beat faster as each child wondered which of these he would receive.

At last Mr. Jellicoe arrived, a short, bald, and immensely stout man who was much given to laughter. There was great excitement as he began to award the prizes—a book for one, a medal for another, a blue or gold ribbon for a third. Young Clark himself was awarded a copy of

Shakespeare's plays. He had shown remarkable talent in composition and had the highest marks in English Literature. He had even begun to have thoughts of making his living later on as a writer—a novelist, perhaps, or a playwright, or what was even more exciting, a reporter.

As he returned to his desk, carrying the book Mr. Jellicoe had just given him, he heard Miss Lang say, "That's strange, Mr. Jellicoe. I'm sure it was here."

"I don't see it," Mr. Jellicoe said.

"Then it must still be in the desk," Miss Lang answered. "I'll get it."

She opened the drawer of her desk and began searching for something. Mr. Jellicoe went on handing out the awards, occasionally casting an anxious glance in Miss Lang's direction.

It was at this moment that the strange thing happened.

Clark watched the teacher as she poked about in the desk drawer, and as he did so he became slowly aware that he was also looking at the inside of the desk, that his eyes had pierced the wood, and that the interior of the desk was quite plain to him. Caught behind the top drawer where Miss Lang could not see it was a blue ribbon.

"Are you looking for a blue ribbon?" Clark asked.

Miss Lang looked up in surprise. "Yes, Clark," she said.

"It's a ribbon for General Excellence," said Mr. Jellicoe. "It's for Lucy Russell. But it doesn't appear to be on the table here. Do you know where it is, Clark?"

"Why, yes," Clark answered. "It's caught behind the top drawer of Miss Lang's desk. If you'll pull the drawer out, you'll—you'll——" He paused and began to falter. The eyes of everyone were upon him, eyes filled with a growing amazement. He realized suddenly that what had seemed to him a natural and ordinary thing was actually most remarkable.

Miss Lang lost no time in pulling out the top drawer of her desk. A moment later she was holding the blue ribbon in her hand. She looked at

Mr. Jellicoe, then at Clark, and then back to Mr. Jellicoe again.

The silence that filled the classroom was almost more than Clark could bear, and he was relieved when Miss Lang said, finally, "How did you know the ribbon was at the back of that drawer, Clark?"

Clark tried to answer but the words would not come. He was as startled as anyone else at what had happened. The simple truth was that he *had looked through the desk* as though the wood were transparent. He was about to say as much when he realized that he would not be believed.

"I—I just knew," he said at last. "I had a—a feeling that—that was the only place the ribbon *could* be."

There were another few moments of silence in which everyone looked at him queerly. Then Mr. Jellicoe frowned and cleared his throat.

"Very strange," he said. *"Very* strange."

The cold, unfriendly tone of Mr. Jellicoe's voice could mean only one thing. Clark looked at Miss Lang. Her mouth was set in a hard, thin line. Even his classmates seemed to shrink away from him. All at once he realized what they were thinking—that he had rummaged through Miss Lang's desk—that he had done a dishonest thing. And there was no way of clearing himself.

When he arrived home puzzled and confused he found a surprise waiting for him. Greeting Eben and Sarah as he came in, he showed them the book he had won.

Eben rose from his chair and put an arm around the boy.

"Son," said old Eben, "ye've done a fine job— a mighty fine job. That book—that book of plays —why, shucks, boy, that's one o' the finest things that's ever happened to yer ma and me. We're proud o' ye!"

Clark looked up at them and felt everything going soft inside him. He loved these two, loved them as nothing else on earth.

Old Eben cleared his throat.

"Yer ma's got a—well, a kinda present fer ye, son. Ye know the masquerade thet's bein' given up to Judge Marlow's place tonight——"

"Yes, I know," said young Clark. "But we decided I couldn't go."

" 'Course ye kin!" cried Eben, slapping him on the back. "It's bein' given in honor of all them young students that won prizes! Ye got t' go!"

"But we talked this all over, Dad!" said Clark. "You said we couldn't afford to rent a costume from the city——"

"That's right, son," Sarah Kent said. "We couldn't afford to rent a costume, but there was nothin' stoppin' me from makin' one—now was there?"

"Get the costume, ma, and let him see it," Eben said.

When Sarah Kent returned with the costume and draped it over Clark's arm, he felt he had never seen anything quite so exciting. There was a tight-fitting suit of blue, a wide belt of leather, knee-length boots, and—most thrilling of all—a scarlet cape. He could hardly wait till he reached his room to try it on.

It took him but a few moments to slip out of

his clothes and into the costume. Arrayed in the blue suit, with the scarlet cape draped from his shoulders, he stood before the mirror and surveyed himself. It was a wonderful costume! And to think that he had not expected to go to the party at all——! He whooped suddenly with delight and leaped into the air, spreading the cape for effect.

The shock of what happened next was almost more than he could bear. He had merely started to jump up and down in his boyish happiness over the costume. When his feet touched the floor again, he was standing *at the other end of the room!*

He stood motionless, staring about him in utter amazement. He could not believe that he had actually flown across the room, and yet——. He decided to try it again. He bent his knees and pushed upward. And then—he was in the air, flying about the room!

He was frightened at first and his heart beat like a triphammer. Just as his eyes could pierce the wood of Miss Lang's desk, so he could fly. What was the answer? How could he do these things when other boys, he knew, could not? Was he different from other boys? He had never thought so before and he didn't want to think so now. He had a feeling that to be different would set him apart, and he saw himself as a queer and lonely figure, shunned by all.

He tried in the months that followed to forget the strange powers he had discovered in himself. Yet as time wore on he would begin to wonder whether he still possessed them, and the temptation would be too great. At such times he would look at whatever was nearest and, using his remarkable vision, see straight through it. At others, when he was sure no one could see him, he would leap lightly into the air and fly about. And after a time, when his fear of these odd things wore off, he came to like them and found joy in practicing them.

As months became years, a superhuman strength was growing in him as well, but he was not aware of it. It was not until he was seventeen that he had his first knowledge of it. It came about in an unexpected way.

The Kent farm had never been successful. Old

Eben was a good farmer and a hard worker, but
as far back as Clark could remember, bad luck
always struck at the very moment when it seemed the Kents were about to find some small
measure of success. About the time Clark reached his seventeenth birthday old Eben found
himself heavily in debt. He told the boy about
it on the eve of the State Fair.

They were standing in the field together.
Eben had finished haying for the day and was
unhitching the old horse in the light of the setting sun. Clark, having completed his chores
about the house, had come to help him.

"Looks like a mighty fine day for the Fair tomorrow," Eben said, gazing off across the fields
to where the sun was dropping behind the hills.

"Yes, Dad, it does," Clark said.

Eben seemed thoughtful and moody, and
Clark knew he had something on his mind. He
would speak of it in his own good time. He did.
He said, finally, "Son, what would ye say if I was
t' tell ye I was thinkin' o' enterin' the Anvil Contest tomorrow?"

Clark straightened up and looked at Eben in

surprise. He could not believe the old man meant it.

"I know it sounds silly to ye, lad," Eben went on, "but we need the money bad! I won the contest once. 'Twas many a year ago when I was a younger man. Still, mebbe I might have a chance. If I can win the prize——"

But how could he hope to win it? Only young men—yes, and only those noted for their strength in the county—ever thought of entering the Anvil Contest. To compete, a man had to grasp an anvil in his arms and lift it from the ground; whoever lifted it highest won $500. The prize had been won the year before by a farmer who, because of his tremendous strength, was locally known as "The Bull." A close second had been Fred Hornbach, whose powerful muscles had made him the champion wrestler of the state. Both were young men, and both would undoubtedly enter the Anvil Contest this year, yet here was Eben Kent, an aging man, proposing to pit himself against two such adversaries. The need for money must be desperate indeed.

It was, as Clark now learned. For the first

time, Eben unburdened himself to the boy, told
him of the unsuccessful struggles of the past
years, and of the inability to make both ends
meet. As the two walked toward the barn, Clark
listened and found growing within him an over-
whelming desire to help Eben Kent.

How he was to do it only time could tell.

CHAPTER IV

THE CONTEST

T HE DAY OF THE State Fair dawned bright and clear, but there was little happiness in Clark Kent's heart. He had slept poorly during the night, his active mind trying vainly to invent some method, to find some way, of helping the aging farmer. He found none, and as dawn broke he sat at his window, looking out across the misty fields, vaguely troubled at thoughts of what the day might bring.

36

After a hearty breakfast, Old Eben and Clark started for the Fair Grounds. Sarah Kent remained at home. The misfortunes of the past years had been harder on her than on her husband, and she had aged, it seemed, much more than he. Fair-going days were over for her, and she preferred now to sit at home.

The Fair Grounds presented a lively sight. Hordes of farmers and their wives and children milled about the various exhibits, and as the sun rose higher and hotter in the heavens the scene became even more hectic. There were competitions of all sorts, prizes given for the finest cows, the best hogs, the sturdiest bulls, the plumpest chickens. There were horse-shoe contests, potato-sack races, all sorts of tests of skill and strength. People filled themselves with hotdogs and ice cream and pickles and a hundred other good things to eat. And everywhere there were laughter and gleeful shouts and the happy din of people who have come to celebrate.

Somehow young Clark and Eben bore the suspense of waiting through the day, for the Anvil Contest was not held until late in the afternoon.

At last, as the shadows lengthened across the Fair Grounds, the crowd began to move toward the platform on which stood the mighty anvil.

The platform itself was decked out gaily with red-white-and-blue bunting. Toward the rear was a bench reserved for the three judges, and to the side another bench where the contestants were to sit. The anvil, newly polished, stood in the very center for all to see.

Clark's eyes roved over the crowd, sought and found what he most feared—the faces of "The Bull" and Fred Hornbach. Throughout the day he had hoped they would not be there, that something might happen to keep them away. He was not disappointed when he saw them, however, for he had felt from the outset that his hopes would be in vain.

Old Eben looked at his son. Clark did not like what he saw in the farmer's face, for one glance was enough to convince him that Eben regretted having come. The old man realized, perhaps for the first time, the impossibility of his winning against such heavy odds. It was too late for him to back down now, however, for his name had been entered on the list, and already one of the judges was beckoning to him to come up on the platform.

"Well, son," he said, "wish me luck!"

"Good luck, Dad!" Clark said, and as he said it he felt empty inside. If only he could help, if only *he* could mount that platform in Eben's place. But how futile that would be! Even now, Fred Hornbach and "The Bull" were taking their places on the side bench, and there was no mistaking the power of their muscles, the strength of their broad backs. Instinctively he felt the muscles of his own arms. Yes, they were strong arms, but they could hardly compare with those of the other two. His heart sank as old Eben mounted the steps.

A ripple of laughter went through the crowd as it caught sight of Eben. Beside the other two he looked indeed a futile, piteous figure. The crowd could not know the desperation that had brought the aged farmer here, could not know the dire need for money that had spurred him to take his chances against impossible odds. It knew only that he looked ridiculous in comparison with the other two.

Clark looked about at the laughing faces and

felt a rage smoldering within him. Jeers and cat-calls were heard as the old man's name was called, and he took his place beside Hornbach and "The Bull." Clark, watching Eben, saw his face flush.

"There's no fool like an old fool," a voice said close to Clark. The owner of the voice was a middle-aged man with graying hair and a face as sour as a lemon. He wore rimless glasses and squinted through them as if he found difficulty in seeing anything even with their aid. He was well-dressed, and it needed but a glance to tell that he was from the city.

Clark glared at the man, who returned the unfriendly stare. He was about to say something, when one of the judges was heard announcing that the contest was about to begin.

The first name called was that of a man who had mounted the platform after Eben. He was not a young man but his strength was apparent. He walked to the anvil and stood over it a moment. Then, amidst encouraging shouts from his friends, he took the anvil in his arms and tried to lift it. Strain and struggle as he might, the anvil would not budge, and he was forced at length to give up.

Fred Hornbach's name was called next. Standing beside the anvil, he spat upon his hands, tightened his broad leather belt about his waist, and waited for the crowd to quiet down. Then he braced himself, his arms about the anvil, and lifted. His face grew dark with the effort it cost him, and the muscles bulged on his arms and neck and shoulders. A roar of approval burst from the crowd as the anvil left the floor. Hornbach held it as the judges quickly measured the distance. One inch. The relief on Hornbach's face was evident as he set the anvil back in its place.

Now came "The Bull"—huge in body, with sturdy legs and a broad muscular back. He was stripped to the waist, and as he approached the anvil the crowd, noting his deep chest, his powerful stomach muscles, the strength of his mighty arms, cheered their champion.

This was "The Bull's" moment, and he did not intend to let it pass quickly. He clasped his hands above his head in the manner of a prize-fighter and turned to all corners of the platform, acknowledging the plaudits of his admirers. As his gaze moved over the crowd it fell upon young Clark. Their eyes met, and the boy disliked the man instantly. There was a smugness in "The Bull's" smile, an arrogance in the curve of his lips, that brought a flush to Clark's face and stirred his heart to anger.

Having given his followers time to admire him, "The Bull" now prepared to lift the anvil. His legs spread wide, his feet firmly planted, he put his arms around the anvil and lifted it from the floor. He seemed to accomplish the feat almost without effort, holding the anvil a good three inches above the boards. He waited till the judges had accurately marked the distance, and then slowly lowered the anvil. Strutting a bit, he returned to his seat amid deafening applause.

Now the name of Eben Kent was called and again a ripple of laughter was heard. Jeers and derisive shouts filled the air as Eben moved toward the anvil in the center of the platform.

"Ye ain't got a chance now, Bull!" somebody called, and the crowd rocked with mirth.

Eben Kent was not a man to be stopped by the

unfriendliness of others. He braced himself, gripped the anvil and, gathering all his strength, heaved mightily. Slowly the laughter died and the cat-calls ceased, for Eben Kent had succeeded in lifting the anvil off the floor and was now straining to win the contest! One inch—two inches—— Clark, watching the old man's face, saw it slowly redden, saw the veins standing out like whipcords on his neck. He felt like screaming, "Put it down, Dad! You'll never make it! You'll kill yourself!" But he could do nothing except stand in the crowd and watch, as Eben Kent refused to own himself beaten and strained in vain to raise the anvil more than three inches from the floor!

A spasm of agonizing pain suddenly shattered the old man's face. He gasped and dropped the anvil. He staggered for a moment—but only for a moment. In the next instant he had straightened up and was smiling gallantly but painfully at the crowd.

Many laughed, for now that Eben had failed he again became for them a ridiculous figure. He was something to laugh at, and the crowd wanted to be amused. Again jeers and cat-calls and derisive remarks were thrown his way. As Eben sat down on the contestants' bench, "The Bull" made a dumb show of being afraid of him, throwing up his arms in mock fear. This was what the crowd wanted and they encouraged "The Bull" to continue. This he obligingly did, to their great delight.

Clark could stand it no longer. Blinded by hot, unreasoning anger he fought his way through the crowd and onto the platform. He stood before "The Bull" with tears of rage streaming down his cheeks.

"Let my father alone!" he shouted. "Let him alone—you hear?"

"The Bull" looked at him in mild astonishment and amusement. He reached out a powerful arm to push Clark away.

"Go 'way, kid, or I'll——"

He never finished what he started to say. As his hand reached out for Clark, the boy stepped aside and swung his fist against the other's jaw. "The Bull" shuddered and sank limply to the floor.

Hardly realizing what he had done, white-hot

anger still seething within him, Clark turned toward the anvil, his eyes blazing. Laugh at his father, would they? He'd show them! He reached down, gripped the anvil in both hands, and lifted. He was almost thrown off balance at the ease with which he raised it and held it aloft, high above his head!

Not a sound, not a breath, came from the astounded onlookers. Clark stood there, looking into the amazed faces of a silent, gaping crowd. And then slowly the wonderment of what he had done came over him. He raised his eyes to the anvil, held aloft in his hands. He shifted it a little to feel its weight. There was no weight. The anvil was like a feather.

He looked toward the other end of the platform. Three of the four contestants, Eben amongst them, were staring at him dumbly. The fourth, "The Bull," lay stretched full-length on the floor. He turned his head still further to where the judges sat. Three pairs of startled eyes were looking at him.

He lowered the anvil to the floor.

And then the crowd went wild!

Shouting and cheering, they surged toward the platform and onto it, milling about the boy. Hands clapped him on the shoulders approvingly and fingers reached out to feel the muscles of his arms.

Questions came from all sides. How had he managed to do it? Had he practiced a long time? What was the secret of such amazing strength?

A middle-aged man with graying hair pushed his way through the crowd to where Clark stood. It was the man with rimless spectacles and the city clothes who had stood beside him not so long ago and called Eben an old fool. He took hold of Clark's arm.

"Young man," he said, "you're what I've been looking for! You're a scoop! I represent the *Daily Planet* in Metropolis. I want the full story of how you developed your amazing strength!"

Clark gulped and seemed unable to find his voice.

"Out with it!" snapped the reporter. "No false modesty now! Give me the story—all of it!"

Clark tried to speak but the words would not come.

"All right, all right, have it your way!" the

The anvil in his hand was like a feather. (Page 45)

man barked. "I'll write the story *my* way! But I'm in your debt, anyway, young man. You've given me the beat I've been looking for all day. If you ever need anything, look me up at the *Daily Planet!*"

He shook the boy's hand and started off through the crowd.

"I don't know your name," Clark called after him.

"Eh?" He paused, squinting back at the boy. "Oh yes. Couldn't very well find me without knowing my name, could you? Well, son, if you ever come to the *Daily Planet* just ask for Perry White. That's all. Just Perry White!"

A moment later he was gone in the crowd.

CHAPTER V

THE DEATH OF EBEN

C LARK KENT never forgot that day, nor the
night that followed. When the wonder of
what he had done abated somewhat and the
crowd began to move off and leave him, he found
his way to Eben who still sat on the contestants'
bench. In his hand Clark held five new one
hundred dollar bills, which the judges had
awarded him, and he was anxious to give these
to the old farmer, happy that a kind, though
rather strange, fortune had given him the chance
to help.

Eben Kent looked up at the boy and tried to smile, but his face was ashen with pain.

"I—I've done somethin'—inside—here," he faltered, pressing his hand against his chest. "We'd—we'd best be gettin' on for home."

Supporting the tired old man, Clark broke a way through the crowd. Five miles or more lay between them and home. They had walked the distance that morning, but Clark knew Eben would never be able to walk it now. How right he was he did not know until they reached the narrow wagon-road that led to the Kent farm. Here Eben suddenly went limp in the boy's arms, and Clark knew he had collapsed.

Clark looked about him. There was no one in sight. Speed was vital. He must get to the farm quickly and call a doctor. There was no time to waste. And so now he did what he had never attempted before. He lifted Eben Kent in his arms as easily as if he were a child and, like a bird, left the ground.

Sweeping through the air, with the old man cradled in his arms, the full realization of his powers dawned on him. Up to now this curious ability of his to fly, to see through things—this wondrous strength discovered only that that afternoon—all these had seemed like strange playthings, not to be taken seriously. But now, as he sped through the air, he knew suddenly that he was a man apart, that he was not like ordinary men, that he was a super-being. He understood more than this. He understood that these miraculous powers could be harnessed and put to use. If a man could fly, if his eyes were gifted with X-ray vision, if he possessed the strength of countless men—what could he not do? He turned these things over in his mind as he flew toward home.

Once arrived at the farm, he quickly summoned the local doctor. Clark and Sarah Kent waited anxiously while the doctor completed his examination of Eben. At last he finished and joined them in the parlor.

"Well?" Clark questioned anxiously. "What is it, doctor?"

The gray-haired physician placed his instrument bag on the table.

"It isn't easy to tell you this, Sarah, or you,

son, but lifting that anvil, I'm afraid, was too much for Eben's heart—more than it could stand. I could put it into scientific language for you, but—well—the simplest way to say it is that he used up all his strength. I—well, frankly—I don't expect him to last the night."

When the doctor had left, Sarah Kent went into the room where Eben lay. She was with him a long time. When she came out, Clark saw that she had been crying, even though now her eyes were dry.

"He wants to see you," she said.

Clark nodded and entered the room.

Eben lay propped up in bed. Against the white pillows his face was haggard and drawn with pain. He smiled wanly as Clark entered the room. He motioned the boy to a chair near the window through which a setting sun was sending its last, weak rays.

"Dad——" Clark began, but the old man raised a restraining hand.

"There's not much time, lad," he said, "so I'll do the talkin'."

He leaned back against the pillows and re-

The steel bullet went hurtling into space. (Page 19)

garded Clark with a sad smile. For some moments he lay thus without saying a word. Then he began to talk. As he talked the shadows deepened in the room as the sun sank lower behind the hills. The western sky became a blazing flood of color. Then the colors began to fade, melting into each other, blending at last into a somber gray. And the old man talked on, telling the boy the story of how he had been found and adopted, of his early years, of the mystery that surrounded his life before the arrival of the miniature Space Ship on earth.

"And now ye know," he said at length. "Lad, ye have within ye powers there's no explainin'. Ye're a—a modern miracle, that's what ye be. 'Tis not for you nor me to question the ways of God." He raised himself against the pillows. "But these powers ye have, lad, and it rests with you whether ye'll put them to good use or to bad!"

Clark said nothing. He sat looking out at the western hills, tears burning his eyes. Old Eben went on.

"Let me guide ye, son, as I have these seventeen years. There's great work t' be done in this world, and you can do it. Ye must use these powers of yours to help all mankind. There are men in this world who prey on decent folk—thieves, murderers, criminals of every sort. Fight such men, son! Pit your miraculous powers against them! With you on the side of law and order, crime and oppression and injustice must perish in the end!"

Clark sat and said nothing and the shadows deepened in the room.

"One thing more——" Old Eben's voice came feebly out of the growing darkness.

"One thing more. Men are strange. They believe the wrong things, say the wrong things, do the wrong things. 'Tisn't that they want to, but, somehow, they do. They'd not understand ye, lad. 'Tis not given me t'say how they'd act toward ye, but I know it would not be in the right way."

He took a deep breath before going on.

"So ye must hide your true self from them. They must never know that you're a—a superman. Aye, ye must hide yerself from 'em——"

His voice trailed off oddly.

"Ye must hide yerself—from—'em——"

Clark leaped from the chair to the bedside, and his arms were around the old man in an instant.

"Dad——" he choked.

"Listen to me, son." Clark could barely hear the words and bent his ear close to old Eben's mouth. "It strikes me now. I called ye a—a superman, and that's what ye be. Remember that. You're *Superman!*"

Once again, for the second time that day, Eben Kent went limp in Clark's arms. But this time was the last. No need for words now. Clark left the room. Sarah Kent was waiting outside. Their eyes met. Without a word she stepped into the room and closed the door behind her.

Clark walked to the front door, opened it, and went out into the cool, night air. Stars were twinkling now in the blue vault of the heavens. He started across the fresh-turned fields, the smell of the earth in his nostrils, the damp air against his cheeks. He never knew how long or how far he walked. He only knew that when finally he sat down on the brow of a lonely hill, with nothing about him but the quiet moonlit land, he had decided definitely what he must do, what course his life must take.

CHAPTER VI

CLARK KENT, REPORTER

YEARS PASSED before Clark Kent took advantage of the invitation given him by the newspaperman, Perry White. During that time he became more and more aware of his miraculous powers. Soon he realized that he was indeed a superman, and that he was capable of doing things no other person on earth could do.

The realization carried with it great responsibility. He told himself that he must not let these marvelous powers go to waste, that he must put them to their fullest use. He pondered over Eben's last words to him and reached the conclusion that the old man had been right. The one way in which he might best use his superhuman talents was in service to mankind. Having decided on this, he dedicated himself to combating evil and injustice in all their forms and wherever they appeared.

It was not as Superman, however, that he presented himself one morning at the offices of the *Daily Planet* newspaper in the city of Metropolis. Although he had adopted as his Superman costume the blue suit and flowing red cape that Sarah Kent had once made for him, he was careful to keep it well concealed under his ordinary business clothes. Remembering Eben Kent's advice, he made certain that no human being ever became aware of his double identity.

So it was that a tall, handsome, but rather quiet-mannered young man wearing horn-rimmed spectacles walked into the offices of the

Daily Planet, introduced himself as Clark Kent, and inquired mildly if he might see Perry White. He was surprised to learn that Perry White was now editor of the *Daily Planet,* one of the great-est newspapers in the country.

"No, Mr. White isn't expecting me," he re plied in answer to a secretary's questioning, "but just tell him that Clark Kent is here. I'm sure he'll remember me and want to see me."

The girl motioned him to a seat and disap-peared through a door marked *Private.* As the door opened and closed a voice blasted forth briefly.

"Who's running this paper, Lois—you or I? By Harry, I tell you——!"

Kent had heard enough to recognize Perry White's gruff, perpetually angry voice. He might have heard more, possessing, as he did, the abil-ity to hear through walls and across vast distances —but he was careful to keep his strange talents in check and never listened or looked when he felt he should not.

As he waited, the door from the hallway open-ed and a man entered.

"White in?" he asked, addressing himself to Clark.

Instinctively Kent did not like the man's looks. He was small and thin and his face reminded Kent somehow of a weasel's. He was expensively but not tastefully dressed, his clothes having the appearance of fitting him too well. Kent sensed at once that there was something sinister about the man. His eye caught a bulge in the right-hand pocket of the stranger's jacket. Using his super-vision, he was startled by what was revealed to him. The bulge, he saw, was made by an automatic revolver!

He was about to reply to the other's question, when the door to Perry White's office swung open and the editor's secretary came out.

"I'm sorry, Mr. Kent," she said, "but Mr. White can't see you. He's in conference."

Kent looked at the girl in surprise.

"But he told me to come and see him," he said. "I know it was years ago, but——"

The girl interrupted.

"I'm sorry," she said. "The truth is Mr. White doesn't recall your name at all."

The realization that Perry White did not re-

member him was a disappointment. He understood immediately, however, that it was no fault
of White's. In the years that followed Clark
Kent's boyhood feat with the anvil, Perry White
must have encountered many stories just as exciting and thrilling. It was reasonable that he
should forget the name of the boy whom he had
once told to come and see him at any time.

Kent thanked the girl and turned to leave. As
he moved toward the door leading to the hallway, the little man with the flashy clothes brushed by him. He heard him say: "I wanna see Mr.
White."

Kent opened and closed the door behind him
without listening for the secretary's reply. Something, however, made him turn and make use of
his super-vision to peer back into the room
through the wooden door. The gun in the man's
side-pocket worried him and he wanted to be
sure there was nothing wrong before leaving.

It was fortunate that he did turn, for he was
just in time to see the man push White's secretary aside with the words "Outta my way, sister!"
and throw open the door to the editor's private
office.

Perry White, older and grayer, but still wearing rimless spectacles, sat behind a desk and looked up as the man entered. Seated in a chair before the desk was a slim, dark-haired girl. Kent was hardly aware of these things, however, for his eyes were fixed on the gun hand of the weasel-faced intruder. The man's right hand had slipped into his jacket pocket, and when it came out again it was holding the revolver.

He heard the man say, quietly: "You don't know me, do you, White?"

Perry White, who had half-risen from behind the desk, and whose eyes also were glued to the gun, shook his head slowly and tried to speak, but the words would not come.

"Then I'll tell you who I am," the man said. "A friend of mine went to the electric chair last night. Frankie Gondero—remember?" White nodded slowly, and when the man spoke again his voice was cold as steel. "You and your paper sent him there. You started the investigation, dug up the evidence, testified in court. What happened? They sent little Frankie to the chair."

The speaker paused, his eyes piercing and holding White's own. Then he wet his lips and went on.

"I'm Frankie Gondero's brother. I swore I'd get you, and that's why I'm here. Say your prayers, White. I never miss."

Kent, peering through the door to the hallway, saw the girl who sat before the editor's desk turn pale as her hands tightened on the chair. White started to say something, but the killer cut him short.

"I didn't come here to listen to any stories. Frankie's dead—and so will you be, White, in just two seconds!"

In what seemed like a split second Clark Kent was standing on the threshold of the private office. The little man swung around sharply.

"Shut that door!" he snapped.

"Yes, sir, I—that is——" Kent faltered.

"Shut it!"

Kent closed the door with a hand that shook visibly. He was playing his part well. He turned toward the killer, his face a study in fear.

"I—I don't know what—this is all about," he

stammered. "I just came back to—to see Mr. White and—and——"

"Come here!"

Gondero motioned Kent toward him with the gun. Kent approached timidly. Gondero's lips curved in a sneer.

"Keep coming," he said. "I'm not taking any chances."

"You're a fool," Perry White muttered. "You can't get away with this!"

"Don't worry about me," Gondero answered, watching all three people with a wary eye. "I won't get caught, because I don't expect to leave here alive. When I've finished with the three of you——"

"The three——?" Perry White stopped, staring at the man in disbelief. "You can't kill these people! They've done nothing. Kill me, if you want to, but this girl had nothing to do with sending your brother to the chair, and neither did that young man. I don't even know who he is!"

"If I kill you I might as well kill us all. What's the difference?"

"You're crazy! You're out of your mind!"

Gondero laughed. It was a short, queer laugh.

"Sometimes I think I am," he said. His voice hardened again. "You!" he snapped, motioning to Kent with the gun. "Turn around!"

It was exactly the moment for which Kent had been waiting. As he turned he staggered as though he were about to collapse. He fell forward, throwing his arms about Gondero's neck, his body pinning the gun between the two of them.

Cursing, Gondero struggled to free himself. Kent heard White shout: "Look out, Lois, I'll handle this!" The gun went off several times and Kent felt the bullets strike his chest harmlessly. Then he slumped to the floor, dragging Gondero with him. With a well-concealed movement he sent the gun flying from the would-be killer's hand as they fell.

The sound of shots brought people running from the outer room. In a few moments Gondero was a prisoner. He was led away, vowing vengeance against Perry White. It was time, Kent decided, for him to regain his senses. He moaned slightly and opened his eyes.

"Young man," White cried, helping him to his feet, "I'm in your debt." Exactly the same words, Kent recalled with a smile, that White had used to him years before.

"What—what happened?" he asked.

"You fainted, that's what happened."

It was the voice of the dark-haired girl, and Clark thought he detected a note of sarcasm in it. He looked toward her and saw that she was regarding him with a scornful smile. He knew at once that she thought him a coward. Well, that was the part he must play.

"I—I'm sorry," he faltered. "Guns always make me nervous."

"And why shouldn't they?" White demanded. "I'm glad you're nervous, I'm glad guns frighten you, I'm glad you fainted. If you hadn't we'd all be dead now. I want to shake your hand. Who are you, young man, who are you?"

"I'm Clark Kent. Your secretary said you couldn't see me, but I came back, thinking you might give me an appointment."

"Of course I'll give you an appointment—and right now!" The editor's face almost beamed with pleasure. He took Kent by the arm and led him to a chair beside the desk. "Sit down," he said, "do sit down." He turned to the others who still crowded the office. "And you," he bellowed, "get out! What do you mean, barging into my office this way? Get out—y'hear?—get out!"

In a few moments the office was empty, except for White, Kent, and the girl.

"You'd better go too, Lois," White said. "I'll talk to you about that other matter later."

"All right."

She paused at the door and glanced over her shoulder.

"If our young hero is looking for a job as a reporter he should be good at digging up material for the Women's Page."

She smiled derisively, turned on her heel, and went out.

"Don't mind Lois," Perry White said. "Sarcasm is her middle name. Do you want a job as a reporter?"

"I'd like nothing better, Mr. White."

The editor regarded him thoughtfully.

"I certainly owe you something for saving my

life," he said finally. "But a job as a reporter—well, I don't know. Ever written anything?"

"Nothing to speak of, sir," Kent said.

"Hmmmm. That makes it difficult, you see. Can't take chances on an unskilled man. Still, maybe we might be able to train you."

"All I ask is a chance," Kent said.

"And I'd certainly like to give it to you," White replied, rubbing his chin in a thoughtful, puzzled way. "Trouble is, though, I can't take chances with an inexperienced——. Wait a minute!" He struck the desk with the palm of his hand. "I've got it! The very thing!"

He searched hurriedly through some papers on his desk and finally found what he was looking for, a long sheet of heavy yellow paper. He handed it to Kent who saw that it contained a number of short items teletyped, apparently, from one of the news services.

"That item there," said White, pointing to a paragraph in the center of the page.

Kent read it.

BOLTON, ME. (SPECIAL SERVICE)——
REPORTS CIRCULATED HERE TODAY THAT

THE NANCY M, A CLIPPER SHIP LOST IN
A STORM AT SEA TWO CENTURIES AGO,
HAS BEEN SEEN BY WORKERS AT THE
LOWELL SHIPYARD. SOME EYEWITNESSES
CLAIM THAT THE PHANTOM SHIP IS
MANNED BY A SKELETON CREW.

"Well, what do you think of it?" White asked.

"I'm not quite sure, Mr. White."

Perry White pulled his chair closer to Kent's. "I've always played hunches," he said, "and I've got a hunch there may be something in this Skeleton Ship story. It's not a good enough hunch, though, for me to send a valuable man all the way to Maine to look into it." He sat back and regarded Kent with a quizzical smile. "How would *you* like to go?"

Kent looked at the editor in mild surprise.

"I mean it," said White. "It'll be good experience for you and it'll prove whether my hunch is right or wrong. I'll put you on a small salary, and if you make good—if you manage to dig up the kind of story I'm looking for—I'll make you a full-fledged reporter when you get back. Will you accept?"

Would he accept!

Clark Kent left the offices of the *Daily Planet* with the feeling that he was walking on air. That feeling, he reminded himself with a smile, was not too unusual for him

CHAPTER VII

THE SKELETON SHIP

A SINISTER GRAY FOG shrouded the Maine shipyard, hung from the spars of creaking ships like tattered banners. Somewhere in the sleeping town behind the shipyard a steeple clock tolled the hour of eleven, and off in the distance a foghorn mourned sorrowfully.

A close observer of the scene might have noticed a man standing in the fog—a tall man dressed in dark gray. The man was Clark Kent. He stood at the beginning of a pier that jutted out into the mist-choked river. He had not moved for over an hour, remaining perfectly motionless so that in his gray garb he had indeed become part of the fog itself.

Such was his intention, for he wanted to see without being seen. Something was about to happen, though what exactly it might be he could not foretell. It would be something sinister and fraught with danger, this much Kent knew. And he waited now as the clammy fog swirled around him and the last note of the steeple clock echoed through the darkly glistening streets of the town behind him.

Then it came! His keen ears picked up the sound at the other end of the long pier. His body stiffened. Something had moved at the end of that pier, something that had no business being there. For the first time in over an hour Kent stirred, slipping silently into the fog in the direction of the sound. He did not bother to remove his ordinary clothes to reveal the scarlet cape and blue suit he wore beneath them. For, as he told himself with a grim smile, this was not yet a job for Superman.

He had taken only a few steps when he stopped suddenly. The thing at the end of the pier had moved again. Kent waited, listening. The sound was not repeated. He heard nothing now but the creaking of ships that rode at anchor, the lapping sound of the dark river water against the pilings, and the muffled moan of the foghorn off in the channel. Once more he slipped forward through the fog.

Then came a hoarse cry—a cry for help. Hurtling forward, Kent stripped off the everyday clothes of the meek, mild-mannered reporter. Superman was needed now—and it was as Superman, in flaming red cape and blue tights, that he reached the scene of action!

His piercing eyes saw and understood the situation in a flash. Three mysteriously robed and hooded figures were advancing on an old, white-bearded man who retreated before them to the edge of the pier. And in the flash it took Superman to size up the situation, he also saw the Old Man slip on the wet edge of the pier, strike his head and fall backward into the water, clutching at thin air.

Superman leaped forward, his mighty arm sweeping aside the three cowled figures. Over the side of the pier he went, cleaving the water in a perfect dive. Under the surface his eyes sought and found the limp form of the Old Man as it sank through the murky depths. His arms were about the unconscious figure in an instant and a mighty surge of his powerful legs brought them both to the surface. The next moment they were on the pier again and Superman was desperately beginning the job of fanning into flame the spark of life that still remained in the Old Man's body.

As he worked over the wet, seemingly lifeless form, the fog thickened and the moaning horn off in the channel took on a more somber note. It was not until the town clock struck the half-hour and its mournful echo wandered through the empty streets of the town like some lonely ghost, that the Old Man gasped, opened his eyes, and then started up in sudden fear.

"It's all right," said the higher-pitched voice

of Clark Kent, for Superman had assumed again his disguise of the mild-mannered reporter.

The fear died slowly in the Old Man's eyes, and his bony fingers relaxed their grip on Kent's shoulder.

"Who are ye?" The Old Man's voice bore the unmistakable twang of a Yankee accent.

"Clark Kent's my name. I'm a newspaper reporter. Who are you and who were those men who almost succeeded in killing you?"

"Men?" the Old Man echoed. "Have they gone?"

Kent nodded. "Disappeared in the fog. Who were they and why did they gang up on you?"

The Old Man regarded Kent queerly.

"Didn't ye—didn't ye see their faces?"

Kent shook his head.

"No," he said, "their backs were toward me and they wore hooded robes. What about their faces?"

"That's it." The Old Man's eyes narrowed. "They didn't have none!"

Kent, wondering whether the Old Man was crazy, said nothing but waited for him to go on.

And as he waited he suddenly sensed danger. He could never explain these premonitions, but he trusted them implicitly. Somehow a different note had crept into the banshee wail of the fog-horn off in the channel, and the thickening fog had become like a thing alive, its clammy fingers plucking at his face.

The Old Man did not continue, but merely sat staring off into the distance.

"You say they had no faces?" Kent prompted.

"No faces," the Old Man echoed. He turned his gaze slowly on Kent. "That is, not human faces. They were skeletons!"

Again he paused, staring off into the fog, and after waiting a reasonable length of time, Kent said: "Look here, sir, I wish you'd start at the beginning. There are a lot of things I don't understand, things I'd like explained. First of all, who are you? And what were you doing out here on the pier at this strange hour?"

The Old Man looked at him intently for a long time before replying. Then he said: "Ye saved my life, lad, and I'd like to trust ye—but I daren't! 'Twould be fatal for both of us if I

Superman brought the Old Man to the surface. (Page 76)

was to tell ye who I am and what I do here." He stopped Kent's protest with an uplifted hand. "Ye'll know all in good time—but not now. I cannot trust ye, lad, but I must ask ye to trust me."

Kent nodded. "I trust you. But you can at least tell me about those men. They had the faces of skeletons, you say?"

The Old Man nodded.

"Aye," he said. "They're from off the ship."

"What ship?" Kent asked.

"The Skeleton Ship," came the reply, "the Nancy M."

Again there was silence between them. The foghorn moaned its eerie note, the boats at anchor creaked mysteriously, and the fog wrapped itself about the two figures on the pier like some great gray cape. The clock in the town struck the three-quarter hour. Kent raised his head slowly. Once more he had caught that strange scent of impending danger. Something was going to happen and it was going to happen soon.

The Old Man was saying:

"If ye're a reporter, lad, ye're here doubtless t'find out what ye can about the Skeleton Ship. Do ye know the story of the Nancy M?"

"No," Kent said. "I wish you'd tell me."

"I will," said the Old Man. He began: "Two hundred years ago this little town was a thriving seaport. Clipper ships left this pier we're sitting on, bound for the spice lands of China and Arabia and India—all the ports of the Seven Seas. Sometimes, as ye'll understand, they didn't return." He paused and raised his head, cocking it to one side. He seemed to be listening for something. After a time he went on.

"One of the finest ships o' that time was the Nancy M, a full-rigged schooner owned and captained by Joshua Murdock. Nancy Murdock was his wife and the ship had been named after her."

The steeple clock in town struck the hour of midnight. The Old Man waited till the last ominous note had died before he continued.

"Joshua Murdock's wife had a dream the night afore his last sailing. The dream affrighted her so that she begged her husband not to leave. He laughed at her fears, o' course, but to quiet her he promised no matter what happened he would return. Ye must know, lad, that Joshua Murdock was never known to break a promise. Well, sir, the ship went down in a storm while rounding the Horn and all hands was lost."

The Old Man paused again. Kent said, "Then you mean that this ship—this Skeleton Ship——"

The Old Man nodded. "Joshua Murdock promised his wife to return. And that he does, even though he sails a ghost ship with a skeleton crew. Ye see, lad——"

He broke off suddenly as a strange sound came out of the night.

"Steady," Kent whispered.

They both had heard the single hollow footstep at the same time. It came again. Someone was moving toward them from the end of the pier with slow and measured tread.

A slight breeze had sprung up and the fog began to move like some great gray monster stirring in its sleep. Through the shifting pall the footsteps echoed nearer.

And then out of the swirling fog he came,

walking slowly, head bent as if in thought—a tall broad man dressed in the garb of two centuries ago. Sensing the presence of Kent and the Old Man, he stopped.

"You——" Kent challenged. "Who are you?"

The stranger looked up. The Old Man uttered a low cry and slumped into Kent's arms. For it was no face at all that the man had raised to them, but the death's-head of a skeleton.

"You ask my name?" he said. "It is Captain Joshua Murdock."

He began to laugh quietly, and raising the fleshless index finger of his right hand, pointed through the fog in the direction whence he had come. And the sound of his hollow laughter seemed to roll back the fog, for Kent, looking beyond him to the end of the pier, saw a ship tied alongside where there had been no ship before. And leering down at him from the wooden rail were the skeleton faces of a skeleton crew—— the crew of the Nancy M!

*Leering down at Kent were skeleton faces
of a skeleton crew.* (Page 84)

CHAPTER VIII

THE VANISHING CAPTAIN

T HE WEIRD FIGURE of Captain Joshua Murdock stood not ten feet in front of Kent,
pointing with bony finger to where the Skeleton Ship was tied to the pier, skeleton seamen
leering down from the rail. In his arms Kent
held the limp figure of the Old Man. The fog
had in this brief instant become thick again, rolling in smoke-like waves across the scene, so
that even now it was obscuring the Skeleton Ship
and its grisly crew. Kent knew he must work
fast—and did!

He let go of the Old Man, who groaned as he slipped to the dock planking. Quickly Kent moved toward the skeleton figure of Captain Murdock. It was the very quickness of his movement that resulted in failure, for as he started forward something wrapped itself around his ankles and he went down!

He was up instantly, but in that fraction of lost time the scene had become again what it had been before. Fog—nothing but gray, swirling fog. The horn, moaning off in the channel. The faint creaking of ships at anchor. Of the Skeleton Ship there was not a trace, and Captain Murdock had vanished completely.

Kent looked down to see what had caught at his ankles and sent him sprawling. It was the arms of the Old Man. Somehow, as Kent let him slip down, his arms had fallen about Kent's ankles, causing the young reporter to trip as he moved suddenly forward.

Clark Kent did not believe in ghosts, yet he could not deny what he had just seen with his own eyes. There was no doubt that the Skeleton Ship was the Nancy M, for he had seen the name in worn, discolored letters on the bow. She had all the tragic marks of a sunken ship, for her canvas hung in tatters, her spars lay tangled and splintered, and her entire hull was covered with barnacles and coral, showing that she had lain for a long time at the bottom of the sea.

As for the crew that lined the rail, he was convinced they were skeletons. His vision was superior and he trusted without question the evidence of his own eyes. Those men *were* skeletons. He had seen the empty sockets of their eyes, the glistening jawbones, the fleshless joints of their fingers as their arms rested on the ship's rail.

Captain Murdock was something else again. Kent couldn't exactly say why, but there was something—well, unreal—about him. The bony finger with which he had pointed toward the ship had not seemed to be bone at all. The same held true for his skeleton face. No, there was something not quite genuine about Captain Joshua Murdock, and Kent made up his mind to find out what it was.

The Old Man moaned and stirred at Kent's

feet. As Kent lifted him from the dock, holding an arm about him to keep him from falling, the Old Man looked up questioningly.

"You—you saw it?"

"Yes, I saw it."

"Then it's true," the Old Man said. "There *is* such a thing as the Skeleton Ship!"

"I don't know yet," Kent said.

"But you saw it! It was there!"

Kent shook his head. "It was there, and yet it wasn't there. There's a Skeleton Ship, yet there isn't a Skeleton Ship."

"Just what do ye mean by that?"

The Old Man's wrinkled face was close to Kent's, his small eyes peering intently into Kent's own.

"What do ye mean?" he repeated.

"I don't exactly know," said Kent at length. "Not yet, at any rate."

Kent looked about him. The fog still rolled in heavily from the channel and the horn still moaned out its warning to ships at sea. The steeple clock off in the dark, echoing town struck the quarter hour. But the air of mystery and expectancy which had gripped Kent before was no longer there. The thing had already happened; there would be no further adventure on the pier that night.

"Look here," Kent said, "there's nothing more to be done here. I'm going back to my hotel. What about you?"

"Don't ye fret none about me," said the Old Man. "Just ye leave me bide here. I'll be all right."

Kent shook his head. "I'm not so sure about that. You almost lost your life a while back."

"That won't happen again," the Old Man replied. "I'll know what t'expect from here on. You go along. I'll be all right."

"As you wish," said Kent, and turned to go. He paused for a moment. "Are you sure you can't tell me who you are?" he asked.

The Old Man stared at him a brief instant. Then he reached out and took Kent's hand in his.

"Lad," he said, "we've both got a job to do here, and we're in this together. As for who I am, it don't matter. Ye'll understand everything some day. Before that day comes, you and me'll see a lot o' dangers. Mebbe we'll live through 'em, mebbe we won't. But all I can say to ye now is—don't ask any questions.''

Kent returned the friendly pressure of the Old Man's hand.

"I'll trust you," he said. Turning, he walked off toward town.

On his way to the waterfront hotel where he had engaged a room, Kent decided to walk past the grounds of the small estate of John Lowell, owner of the local shipyard. He had made a point of meeting Mr. Lowell at the shipyard that morning, had told him who he was and what he wanted to do, and had received the owner's permission to investigate matters as he saw fit. Lowell, a small, sallow-faced man nearing fifty, gave evidence of the strain of the situation in which he found himself and was anxious for whatever help he could get. Kent hoped that the shipyard owner might still be up and about. He wanted to tell him what had happened that night and discuss it with him.

Arriving at the gate of the iron fence that surrounded the estate, Kent saw lighted windows shining through the murk. He was in luck. Lowell, apparently, had not yet retired for the night.

Kent thrust open the gate and entered the grounds. Walking up the winding, pebbled path that led to the front door, he was again assailed by that strange sense of impending danger. It was so strong, in fact, that he stopped short, listening, waiting, trying to feel the texture of the atmosphere about him.

Here as elsewhere the fog hung thick and clammy. The trees were weird figures when seen through the mist, some gnarled and twisted and waiting like sentries, others towering through the murk with wide-spread clutching arms. Sounds came through the fog—mysterious little sounds that told of numberless insects that crawled and flew about through the trees. A bull-frog croaked from the swampy depths of a near-by pool, and in one of the trees an owl hooted sorrowfully.

Kent paused only for a moment and then, shrugging his shoulders, went on. Reaching the house, he went up to the front door and rang the bell. Through the leaded bay window that gave on the lawn, he could see John Lowell seated behind the desk in his study, going over accounts by the light of a desk-lamp. The door opened and an elderly woman in a black house-keeper's dress stood in the yellow light that shone from within.

"Yes?" she said.

"I'd like to see Mr. Lowell," Kent said. "I know it's late, but I think he'll see me. Please tell him that Clark Kent is calling."

"Come in, please," she said. "I'll tell Mr. Lowell you're here."

She returned in a few moments and led Kent into the study, where Lowell rose from his desk to greet him.

"I didn't expect to see you again so soon," he said in a dry, nasal voice. "Has anything happened?"

"Yes, something has," Kent replied.

"Sit down and tell me about it."

Kent told the weird story from beginning to end. Lowell was silent for a long time after Kent had finished. Finally he said: "You believe it was a Skeleton Ship you saw?"

"I'm sure of it," Kent replied.

The shipyard owner nodded and sat for a few moments deep in thought. Then he rose and moved toward the window where he stood looking out into the fog-shrouded night. When he spoke again, his voice was low and filled with all the worry and perplexity this strange situation had brought on him.

"I didn't believe it at first," he said. "When the night watchman was found wandering about the pier and babbling insanely, I refused to believe. When several of the men on the night shift saw the ship and walked out, followed by the others, I still couldn't believe that such a thing was possible. That a clipper ship and its crew, at the bottom of the sea for over a century, could return—no, it was ridiculous even to think of it."

"I can understand your feelings," said Kent.

"I spent nights on that pier myself," Lowell continued. "I wanted to see it with my own eyes. Nothing ever happened. But now you tell me you have actually seen it! Somehow I believe you. You impress me as a man not easily fooled."

He started, peering intently through the window. "What the devil——!"

Kent was at his side immediately.

"What is it?"

Lowell shook his head and grinned sheepishly.

"Sorry, Mr. Kent, but I'm afraid my nerves are getting jumpy. I thought for a moment I saw a man walking out there under the trees. The fog plays strange tricks at times."

He sat down again behind the desk, and began to fill a pipe with nervous fingers. Kent glanced briefly through the window, but saw nothing.

He was about to say as much when the door from the entrance-hall was opened by the housekeeper. As she came into the study, Kent saw that something was wrong. The woman's face was deathly white, and her lips trembled. As she took several steps into the room, she looked back over her shoulder as if she were afraid of being followed.

"What is it, Anna?" Lowell asked.

"There's—there's someone to see you, sir," the woman faltered.

"Send him in."

"He won't come in, sir. Insists that you'll have to come out and see him. He's in the entrance-hall now. If I may say so, sir, there's something very strange about him."

"What do you mean?" asked Lowell.

"I—I can't say, sir. He's a sailorman, and yet— the clothes he's wearing aren't like any I've ever seen before. And there's something about him that—that sends the chills up and down your spine."

The housekeeper shuddered.

"Did he give you any name?"

It was Kent who spoke, and his voice was sharp.

"Yes, sir," replied the housekeeper. "He says his name is Joshua Murdock—Captain Joshua Murdock!"

Kent's eyes met those of Lowell and in an instant both men had brushed by the frightened housekeeper and into the entrance-hall. And then even Kent felt the hair rise at the back of his neck.

The front door was wide open, and through it they could see the black vault of the fog-draped night. They heard the clock strike once in the distance and the far-off muffled moan of the channel-horn.

But the entrance-hall was empty. Captain Joshua Murdock had vanished into the ghostly darkness leaving behind a grim reminder of the sea.

On the floor in the spot where he had stood lay a pile of wet seaweed.

CHAPTER IX
FIRE AT SEA

K ENT, LOWELL and the housekeeper stared in amazement at the pile of seaweed on the floor. Lowell opened his mouth to say something. As he did, the night was pierced by a wail that rose and fell ominously.

"What's that?" Kent snapped.

"Coast Guard siren," Lowell answered. "There's a station near here. Something's happened. I'll have to get down there at once—I'm a member of the Auxiliary."

The housekeeper paled.

"Don't leave me alone here, Mr. Lowell," she pleaded. "There are strange things happening in this house tonight. That seaweed——"

She stared at the dripping pile on the floor, eyes wide with horror.

"Go to your room and lock yourself in, Anna," Lowell said. "There's nothing to fear. Come on, Kent!"

A short time later the two men were speeding to the Coast Guard Station in Lowell's car. They spoke little, each busy with his own thoughts concerning the strange pile of seaweed, seeking explanation as to how it got there, wondering about Captain Murdock, striving to pierce the veil of mystery that enveloped the Skeleton Ship.

Tangled in the mesh of their thoughts was the wail of the Coast Guard siren in the foggy distance. The road they sped along reached and followed the edge of a cliff down to the sea. Looking through the window Kent saw a dull reddish glow far out on the ocean. The reddish glow meant flames, flames meant a burning ship, and Kent knew at once what tragedy had called out the Coast Guard on such a night as this!

Lowell brought the car to a stop in front of the Station. The scene about them was one of feverish activity. One cutter was already a speck on the horizon. A second cutter, twin motors roaring, was headed out to sea. Men worked with furious efficiency readying a third for action. A tall, broad-shouldered officer wearing captain's stripes stepped up to Kent and Lowell.

"Sorry, but——" He stopped short. "Oh, it's you, Mr. Lowell."

The shipyard owner nodded. "Yes, captain. I heard the siren and hurried down. This is a young reporter friend of mine, Clark Kent. Kent, shake hands with Captain Rogers."

The two men gripped hands. "I'm glad you brought Mr. Kent with you, Mr. Lowell," Rogers said. "We're going to need every man we can get. Your station's Number 3, Mr. Lowell. I'll make use of Mr. Kent in a moment."

Lowell hurried off to the third cutter. "That burning ship," Kent said. "What is it, captain?"

"Big oil tanker. She's seventy miles out, wrapped in a pea soup fog. We're going to have trouble rounding up her crew. Wait here a minute. I'll be right back." Rogers vanished into the darkness.

Kent waited only long enough to be certain he was not observed before stripping off his street clothes and revealing the blue and red costume of Superman. There was a job to be done—a job that might be too difficult for the men aboard those cutters.

Seconds meant lives, and only Superman could save those seconds—and those lives!

Faster than a speeding bullet, red cape streaming in the wind, Superman raced out across the dark waters like some giant bird. Straight as an arrow he flew, the reddish glow in the distance becoming ever brighter as he approached swiftly. In a matter of seconds he had passed the slim gray shape of the second Coast Guard cutter cleaving the water far below him, and he smiled in admiration, thinking of the courageous men aboard her, men who challenge any danger and often give their lives that others may live.

It was not until he overtook the first cutter, far ahead of the second and almost at the scene of the tragedy, that his keen ears picked up the sinking tanker's radio signals. What he heard sent him hurtling through the night even swifter, if possible, than before.

The message, halting and broken like the voice of a dying man, read: "Sinking—fast—but —don't—want—help. Submarine—standing—by— in—fog—to—machine-gun—crew—and—sink—assisting—vessels." The message began to repeat. "Sinking fast——submarine—standing—by——"

The signals stopped abruptly, and Superman's jaw set in grim determination as he saw in his mind's eye that gallant radio operator sticking to his post, vainly working a key gone dead. And, oddly, there flashed through his mind all the wonderful stories he had ever heard or read of King Arthur and his bold knights—of daring Launcelot and brave Galahad. And suddenly he laughed aloud. It was a laugh brimming with defiance, the battle cry of a knight who sallies forth to meet the Powers of Darkness!

No prancing white chargers for those men on

the tanker, no burnished shields gleaming in the sun. Their charger was a sinking ship, their burnished shield an oil-flame's glow. Yet they were finer, braver knights than any who had lived before, knights who fought their fight upon a flaming sea!

The scene of action was below him now. A huge inferno of fire to his left marked the stricken tanker. He heard the crackling of the flames, saw men in small boats rowing through a glowing sea. Burning oil covered the water and here and there dark heads bobbed in the liquid fire. The molten air was alive with hoarse shouts and cries of agony.

Standing by, waiting like some great gray monster for the kill, her sides illuminated by the glow of the flaming oil, lay an enemy submarine.

It was the first time Clark Kent had ever seen a sub. What was there about it that seared his veins with white-hot anger? He never knew.

He only knew that he suddenly brimmed with the joy of being Superman and gathered within himself a power of energy that he had never known before.

He went into action as the first Coast Guard cutter shot into the circle of flaming light and reversed her engines to an abrupt halt. Even Superman could never quite recall what happened during the minutes that followed.

As the cutter hove into the scene, the sub let go with a withering burst from a forward gun, to spray the men in the lifeboats with deadly fire. The bullets never met their mark! In the split-second it took to press the automatic trigger of the gun, Superman grasped the situation and in a swooping dive cut across the line of fire! Hundreds of rounds of bullets ricocheted off him harmlessly as, flying low, placing his body between the sub and the small boats, he took the full force of the blast. As he reached the end of his lightning dive, he heard the dull roar of the sub's 6-inch gun, the scream of the shell as it sped toward the cutter, dead on its mark. He turned, hung for a fraction of time like a hawk in flight, and in the next instant caught the white-hot shell in his bare hands! Then his arm, holding aloft the shell, swung back and he hurled the explosive back at the submarine!

The explosion was titanic. The sub reeled over violently as an orange tongue of flame shot high into the air.

The enemy sub was a fighter, however, and Superman was still needed here. Even as the shell crashed into the steel hull, the sub's guns sent round after round into the helpless small boats. Superman dove like a thunderbolt across the raider's bow, and his fist smashed into the machine gun, ripping it from the deck, rendering it into a mass of twisted scrap that spun into the sea! Bolting toward the 6-inch cannon, he swept its crew aside and almost in the same instant crashed his mighty shoulders against the gleaming barrel. The gun had just been fired. Jamming his hand over the muzzle, Superman forced the shell back into the chamber. It exploded inside the gun, splintering the metal into a thousand jagged pieces.

The sub was now listing to port, wallowing like a crippled whale in the trough of the sea. Superman leapt from the deck into the air, turned in mid-flight, and prepared himself for the mighty shock to come. For he knew what must be done, and he knew also that only Superman could do it!

He hunched his shoulders, flexed his mighty muscles, took careful aim, and then—*hurled himself forward!*

He hit the water ten feet from the sub and struck the mighty monster of the deep beneath the water-line! Head, shoulders, and body shattered the metal sides of the craft as if they were made of plywood. On he went, never stopping, coming out on the other side, rising up through the water into the air. He turned again in mid-flight, aimed his body once more, and again bore in under the water-line, piercing the sub at yet another place!

Nor did he stop, until the great gray fish settled to her gunwales and, turning belly upward, sank beneath the waves.

Now he gave his attention to the smoldering inferno about him. The decks of the burning tanker were awash; she wallowed hissing and smoking, as the great fiery seas broke over her. The Coast Guard had done its job well; all hands had been picked up and the tiny boats bobbed on a glowing, empty ocean.

A great wave towered above the crippled tanker that less than an hour ago had been a staunch voyageur of the ocean lanes. Her rudder rose dripping into the air, waving, as it were, a farewell to the life she knew, and then slipped into the ocean depths.

The water boiled over the spot where she went down. Red cape spread to the wind, Superman remained poised for a moment above the foaming circle, saluting silently a monarch of the deep and the men who manned her.

An hour later, Clark Kent sat on the rocky headland, looking out over a sea rosy with the dawn. Below him and to his right was the Coast Guard Station from which he had just come. Lowell, he reflected, had been singularly cool when, arriving with the survivors, he had found Kent still on the pier. Captain Rogers, too, had not bothered to conceal his contempt for (so he thought) the man who had remained behind.

Kent removed his horn-rimmed glasses and began to polish them. Absently moving the handkerchief between thumb and forefinger, he gazed thoughtfully out over the rolling blue of the ocean. Gulls wheeled above him and the air was fresh and salty against his cheek. He recalled that only a few hours ago he had saved the lives of Lowell, Captain Rogers, and the helpless crew of the oil tanker. Yet they all looked at him with frigid eyes. If only he could tell them!

That he was Superman, however, must remain his secret, whatever the cost to Clark Kent. The cost to Kent, he began to realize, would be considerable. He wondered idly about this, wondered too about the connection between the Nazi submarine and the Skeleton Ship. There was some connection, of this he was sure. It was only a "hunch," but he did not possess the brain, the supersensory powers of Superman for nothing.

There would be more submarines, more attempts to sink coastwise shipping, and he must be ready for them.

He smiled. Twenty-four hours had passed since his arrival. Much had happened. Much more would happen before he was through.

CHAPTER X
MYSTERY OF THE OLD MAN

IT BEGAN TO happen, in fact, only a few hours later. Clark Kent was walking along the main street of the seaport town, having just come from the railroad station where he had telegraphed a story of the tanker's sinking to the *Daily Planet*. He wondered, strolling along, what Perry White's reaction to the story would be. He had done his best, but whether Perry White thought his best good enough was another matter.

Leaving the telegraph office, Kent walked out onto the station platform just in time to see a crowded troop train pass through. He reflected idly on where the troops were being moved, and their ultimate destination, as car after car rumbled north.

From the railroad station he started toward the Lowell Shipyard. Crossing the main street, he saw the Old Man he had met the night before standing in front of a ship chandler's shop on the opposite corner. The shop was some distance away, but the sharp eyes of Superman behind the horn-rimmed glasses of Clark Kent could not mistake the shrunken figure, the seedy clothes, the whiskered face.

Kent made up his mind instantly to have a talk with the mysterious Old Man. The tragic events of the night before had strengthened his conviction that there was some connection between the Skeleton Ship and the sinking of the tanker. John Lowell had voiced the suspicion that the Skeleton Ship might be a trick to interfere with war production, to prevent the construction of the hundred PT-torpedo boats he had contracted to build for the government. Kent felt there was more to it than that. If the Skeleton Ship was a trick it was a far too elaborate one for ordinary sabotage. Also, in talking to the telegraph agent, he had learned that five tankers had been sunk off this coast in the last two weeks; the sinking of the first occurred only a few days after the first appearance of the Skeleton Ship. No, he was sure the sinkings were somehow connected with the ghostly appearances of the Nancy M. The Old Man knew something about it, he was sure of that too, and he resolved on the instant to find out what it was.

He crossed the street quickly. As he did so, the Old Man turned from peering into the shop window and began to walk up the street toward him. He had taken only a few steps when he saw Kent coming in his direction. He stopped abruptly, hesitated, and then, turning his back on Kent, began to hurry away. It was obvious that he wished to avoid any encounter with the reporter.

Kent increased his pace. The Old Man reached the chandler's shop and entered. In less than a minute, Kent also reached the door of the shop and went in.

His eyes accustomed themselves quickly to the sudden change from the bright sunlight of the street to the dark, damp interior of the shop. He looked about him. Crowded on all sides, piled in heaps, hanging from every inch of the beamed ceiling, were the countless odds and ends needed in a life at sea. There were binnacles, ropes, compasses, clocks, barometers, lengths of chain. There were maps and charts, telescopes and spyglasses, quadrants and sextants. In brief, there was everything that a sailor could possibly ask for.

From the dark murkiness of the place there came to Clark Kent the tangy odor of brine, a salty coolness, as if the tide had just receded and would in time return and fill the place with sea water.

There was no sign of the Old Man.

Before Kent could decide what to do, a door opened at the rear of the shop and a man came toward him. There was something about the man that exactly fitted the shop and its air of the sea. He was of middle age with a seamed and weather-stained face. He wore dungarees and a gray woolen shirt, and on his head was a seaman's cap. From the corner of his tight, Yankee mouth jutted a short and blackened pipe.

"Ya-ah?" he drawled in a high nasal twang.

"I'm looking for someone who—who doesn't appear to be here," said Kent.

"Sorry," rejoined the other.

"I'm sure I saw him come in here," Kent said. "Maybe you know him—an old man, wearing very old clothes. He's sort of stooped and shrunken."

The other shook his head.

"No," he drawled.

There was a coldness about the man that annoyed Kent.

"Look here," he said, "whether you know him or not, he entered this shop. I saw him come in. You must have seen him!"

"Not me," said the other.

Kent's annoyance was rapidly turning to anger. The Old Man *had* come into this shop, there was no doubt of it. There was no place he might hide, no possible place of concealment anywhere in sight. Yet he was nowhere to be seen, and the man before him claimed he had never set eyes on him. There was something strange here. People did not walk into shops and vanish!

"Listen to me," said Kent. "I saw him come in here, and he must be somewhere in this shop."

"Look fer yerself," said the other.

"That's exactly what I intend doing," Kent replied, "and the first place I'm going to look is behind that door!"

"Hold on!"

There was no drawl in the man's voice now. It was sharp and imperative. Kent, already moving toward the door, drew up. The two men faced each other.

"Yes?" challenged Kent.

The other removed the short black pipe from between his tight lips, and regarded Kent for a moment or two. Then he said: "When I told ye t' look fer yerself, I meant ye might look here— in the front of the store." He replaced the pipe between his yellowed teeth, and added: "There's nothin' back o' that door, nothin' but the lad that assists me."

"Nevertheless," Kent said, "I'll have a look!"

Their eyes met and something in Kent's made the other drop his own. Kent walked toward the door and opened it.

Within, hunched over a worktable repairing a compass, was a young man of about Kent's own age. As the reporter entered, the young man looked up from his work, removed a jeweler's glass from his eye, and smiled genially.

"Hello," he said. "Anything I can do for you?"

For an instant Kent was taken aback. Actually he had expected to find the Old Man in this room, but there was no sign of him, nor was there any other place he might have gone to.

Kent hesitated a moment or two before replying. He was conscious of a strong liking for this young man with the genial smile. He was aware also of something familiar about his face; he had the feeling he had seen that face before.

"I don't know whether you can do anything for me," he said finally. "I'm looking for someone I was sure came in here——"

"Sorry," said the other, "I haven't seen anyone —no one, that is, besides Mr. Barnaby. Oh, Mr. Barnaby——" He addressed the man in the seaman's cap, who had followed Kent into the back room. "Have you seen anyone in the shop?"

Barnaby scowled, took the blackened stump of pipe from his mouth, and said: "No. Told him so. Wouldn't believe me."

"But I tell you I saw him come in here!"

"Ye made a mistake."

Clark Kent had made no mistake. He was sure of that. The Old Man had come into this shop and in the time it took Kent to reach it he had vanished. Even as he talked to Barnaby and the young man, Kent's eyes were roving over the room looking for places where the Old Man might have hidden himself. There obviously were none. There was nothing he could do but accept the word of the other two that the Old Man had not entered the shop at all. He decided to play for time, hoping something might be said, or something happen that would give him a clue.

"Well," he said, "guess I've made a mistake.

Sorry to have bothered you. By the way, I don't believe I introduced myself. My name's Clark Kent. I'm a reporter for the *Daily Planet* in Metropolis."

"Glad to know you," said the young man. "My name's Gorman, Tom Gorman. This is my employer, Mr. Barnaby."

Barnaby acknowledged the introduction with a curt nod.

"A reporter, did you say?" Gorman went on. "What in the world are you doing up here in this forsaken place?"

Kent smiled. "I might ask the same of you," he countered.

Gorman showed his surprise.

"You're right," he said. "I've only been here a few weeks. But how did you know——?"

"For one thing," Kent replied, "you don't sound like a New Englander, and your face is too pale for you to have spent much time in this climate."

His explanation did not hold water and he knew it. On the other hand, he could not tell young Gorman the other things he had noticed.

Gorman's hands, for instance, were slim and white and well-cared for—hardly the hands of a mechanic. There was also the way he held the jeweler's glass in his eye, showing quite clearly that he was not accustomed to it. And there was the impression Kent received as he entered the room, that Gorman was trying to appear busy, that he was just a little too intent upon his work. All in all, though he liked young Gorman, Kent had the definite feeling that here was a man trying to appear what he was not. Then, too, there was that familiar cast to Gorman's face. Where, Kent kept asking himself, had he seen that face before?

Gorman was saying, "I guess you'd call me a rolling stone. I've tried my hand at about every kind of job. Somehow I wound up here. Don't ask me how—it's a long dull story."

On the contrary, thought Kent, he would have found it very interesting indeed. Again he was struck by something odd: Gorman had not been asked for an explanation of his presence here in the chandler's shop; why then did he volunteer one so readily? Why?

Kent stopped asking himself questions, for suddenly he realized why that face was so familiar to him. No, it was not Gorman's face he had seen, but one quite like it—and he had seen it only the night before. He was about to say so when he changed his mind. Gorman would most probably deny any connection, and Kent would only have tipped his hand.

Kent's recognition must have shown itself, however, for Gorman said, "Anything wrong?"

"No," Kent answered. "Just wondering what could have happened to my friend, that's all. By the way, you—er—don't happen to have any close relations in this neck of the woods, do you?"

Gorman looked surprised.

"Relations?" He laughed. "Not that I know of. Why?"

"Nothing, nothing at all," said Kent. "Just wondered." He quickly changed the subject. "I guess I've made a fool of myself insisting that my friend came in here," he said, turning to Barnaby who, all this time, had stood puffing dourly at his pipe and saying nothing. "I'm sorry if I've given you any trouble."

"Fergit it," drawled Barnaby without removing the pipe from between his tight lips.

"Well——" Kent hesitated, "I'll get along."

They said good-by, and Kent made his way out of the shop. On his way through the front part of the store his eyes flickered over every detail of it, searching out a place where the Old Man might be. If he expected to find anything he was doomed to disappointment. There were no unexplored closets, no partitions, no trapdoors. Mysterious though it might be, there was no doubt that the Old Man had entered the ship chandler's shop and promptly vanished!

Walking along the street in the direction of the Lowell Shipyard, Kent pondered the seemingly insoluble problem. It was such problems as this that the mind of Superman delighted in, and he set about taking this particular one apart now, exploring every avenue of solution, examining every angle. It was, after all, as simple as this: The Old Man *had* entered the ship chandler's shop. It would have been impossible for him to have left the shop without being seen by Kent. It would have been equally impossible for him to vanish. There could be only one answer. *The Old Man was still inside the store!*

It seemed the only possible solution, and yet it did not make sense. Well, he must think about it. He must also do some hard thinking about the Skeleton Ship. What was the answer to the ghostly appearance of Captain Joshua Murdock on the fog-shrouded pier the night before? There seemed to be none, strive as he might to pierce the veil of mystery.

One thing he knew. It came to him in a flash. Tom Gorman was related to John Lowell's housekeeper, Anna. That was what had been so familiar about Gorman's face, that was why he thought he had seen it somewhere before. Both faces had similar characteristics, so much so that Gorman and Anna might be brother and sister or mother and son. He wondered if they were. He also wondered why Gorman had denied being related to anyone in town. Gorman, there could be no doubt, was playing a game. Well, Superman would play it with him!

He had now arrived at the gates of the Lowell Shipyard. He paused a moment before going in, and turned to look back in the direction from which he had just come. Through his mind flashed pictures of the Old Man, Tom Gorman, Barnaby, and Anna the housekeeper—and he smiled secretly. Then he thought of the troop train going north that morning, of the thousands of young men on their way to—who could say? The smile vanished from his lips.

He turned the handle of the gate, swung it open, and entered.

CHAPTER XI

ATTEMPTED MURDER

THE SHIPYARD hummed like a beehive. Men hammered and sawed and drilled. Riveters tossed white-hot bolts of metal through the air to be caught and driven home in the skeleton frames of steel ships. Booms swung dangerously through the air bearing girders, super-structures, powerful engines that weighed tons. Flat cars moved in all directions carrying lumber and steel and aluminum. Here and there men swarmed

123

over sleek torpedo boats in the last stages of construction. Activity was everywhere—feverish unceasing activity!

Kent did not go to see John Lowell directly. He chose instead to wander about idly, watching the men at work, keeping a sharp eye open for the clues he sought. Already, he found, he was developing a reporter's view of things, for even as he watched the busy picture about him he tried to put it into words so that it might be included in his next story to the *Daily Planet*. This reminded him that he expected some word from White on his first story and that he must make a point of getting back to the telegraph office before it closed that night.

Moving slowly through the bustling scene about him, he came at last to the pier on which so many strange things had happened the night before. The pier, he now saw, was little used and quite apart from the work of the shipyard, being very old and sadly in need of repair. Hands in pockets, he strolled out onto it casually, not wishing to be noticed by the men at work near by. He wanted to examine the pier carefully and, if possible, find a clue that might lead him to a solution of the mystery of the Skeleton Ship.

The ship had been tied up at the end of the pier, as he recalled, and it was there he went first. Having reached the spot, he paused and tried to figure out what to do next. Had he the slightest inkling of what lay behind the Skeleton Ship, he could have acted accordingly, following some particular line of investigation. The ghostly appearance of the Nancy M, however, was a complete puzzle that offered not even the vaguest of solutions. Search his mind as he might, he could find no answer that made sense.

Pondering, he looked out over the channel, gazing pensively at swirling waters that reflected the slate-colored sky, as if he expected to find in them the explanation he sought. Except for a large sailboat that dipped at a mooring midway between both shores, the waters of the channel were disappointingly empty and gave back no answer to the many questions that filled his brain.

He examined the pier closely, and the more unsuccessful his efforts to find some tell-tale sign to put him on the right track, the more fantastic and unbelievable became the incidents of the night before. Was it really here that he had seen the Nancy M tied up, a skeleton crew grinning down at him from her rail? Did the ghost of Captain Murdock really walk toward him out of the fog at this particular spot? Had any of this actually happened? Or was it—as he was almost inclined to believe—some nightmare of his own, some strange twisting of his imagination?

No, he told himself, these things had happened —and just as there must be a simple explanation for the vanishing of the Old Man in the chandler's shop, so was there a solution to the mystery of the Skeleton Ship. He had only to find the right key, the right clue.

Turning to leave the pier, he saw walking toward him the stocky, gray-haired figure of John Lowell. Keeping pace with Lowell was a thickset man who gave one the impression of having been sprayed from head to waist with a reddish-gold paint. Flaming red hair topped a broad brick-red face, and he wore a bright red shirt which, open at the throat, revealed a thick, florid neck.

"Hello!" greeted Lowell as he came up to where Kent stood. "Any luck?"

"I'm afraid not," Kent replied. He looked inquiringly at Lowell's companion, hesitating to say too much before a stranger. Lowell took the cue.

"You don't have to worry about Slade," he said. "Red's my right-hand man here at the yard."

Kent smiled in spite of himself.

"I figured you'd be nick-named 'Red,'" he said. "I guess Mr. Lowell has told you my name."

"Yeh. Glad t' know ya," rejoined Red.

"You can speak freely, Kent," John Lowell said. "I have no secrets from Red. Uncovered anything?"

Kent shook his head. "Not a thing," he said, "that is, nothing of much value." He was about to divulge his theory of a connection between Anna, the housekeeper, and Tom Gorman, then thought better of it. The information would do Lowell no good at the moment, and he might as well keep it to himself.

John Lowell looked worried. "I wish I could

get to the bottom of this thing quickly," he said. "Just look about you, Kent, and you'll see what this scare has done to my men—even those working on the day shift."

Kent showed his surprise. "I hadn't noticed anything wrong."

Lowell smiled grimly.

"I know," he said. "Things probably look pretty active to you. Well, that's because you haven't seen the yard before, haven't seen the men really working. Red can tell you how much the men are falling down on the job, slowing up, making more and more mistakes. All because they're jittery, Kent—scared to death!"

He looked over the scene for a moment without saying a word. Then he added: "All we need here is an accident—one accident—to make those men throw down their tools and quit for good."

"Awww, stop worryin' about accidents, Mr. Lowell," Slade said. "There ain't gonna be none —don't worry about that."

John Lowell shook his head slowly. "I wish I could be as sure of that as you seem to be, Red," he said, "but too many strange things have happened around here lately for me to feel safe. I've got a feeling inside that—oh, I don't know—a feeling that something may happen at any moment. There's something wrong. The men don't seem to be working right. They—look there!" He pointed to where a heavy boom swung over the hull of a torpedo boat. Swinging slowly from the end of it was a huge engine that looked as though it weighed tons. A man stood below the engine, jockeying it into place with a guide-rope. "Look there," Lowell repeated. "That man's mind is obviously not on his work or he'd be standing to one side of that engine instead of under it!"

"By heaven, ye're right, Mr. Lowell!" cried Red. "That there's a violation o' the rules I laid down. Well, we'll see about this!"

He hurried off to speak to the workman. Kent and Lowell followed slowly.

Halfway across the yard they passed the hulk of an old clipper ship tied up at the abandoned pier, and suddenly Kent saw something that struck him as unusual. He was about to say something to Lowell but decided against it, instinctively disliking to draw attention to a clue until he had made something of it. Suddenly he began fishing through his pockets.

"Lost something?" Lowell asked.

"Yes," said Kent. "I must have dropped my spectacle case, though how in the world I could have done that I don't know. I'd better go back and look for it."

"I'll wait for you here," Lowell said.

It was exactly what Kent wanted him to do, for he wished to examine the ancient clipper ship alone. He began to retrace his steps, only to stop short as a horrified, blood-curdling scream split the air. Turning, he grasped the situation in a flash.

Red Slade, the foreman, was approaching the man who stood under the mammoth engine, jockeying it into position. He apparently had started to give the man a "dressing-down" for his infraction of the rules, when the thing happened. Even as Kent turned, he saw the steel boom sag in the middle, saw the great engine come plunging toward the workman beneath.

There was no time for thought. Action was

needed. Even in his speed Kent noted thankfully that Lowell's back was turned toward him. Faster than a diving fighter-plane, he cleared the air. Gathering momentum as he sped forward, he smashed into the mighty engine. He felt the steel-like muscles of his shoulder sink into the metal, saw the engine hurtle into the deep waters of the channel, and with amazing presence of mind continued on until he swept out of sight behind a near-by machine shop.

An emergency siren was screaming a somewhat futile warning, men shouted in panic, and an ambulance gong was heard in the distance. The shipyard had become bedlam. And silently, unnoticed in the excitement, Clark Kent, bespectacled and mild-mannered, stepped from behind the machine shop and joined the milling throng.

As he forced his way through the crowd to the spot where Red Slade and the workman stood, his quick ears picked up a phrase here, a comment there.

"——a ghost it was!"

"Seen it wid me own eyes!"

Superman felt the steel-like muscles of his shoulder
sink into the metal. (Page 131)

"——like a streak o' light. Don't ast me where it come from!"

"Knocked the engine right into the channel!"

"I'm tellin' ya, this yard is haunted!"

He reached the side of the two men saved from certain, horrible death. John Lowell was already there.

"Kent!" cried Lowell on seeing him. "There you are! Great heavens, man, did you see it? The most amazing—most miraculous—!" He stopped, at a loss for words.

Allayed at once were Kent's fears that any participation in the thing that had just happened might be traced to him. So swiftly had it all transpired that no one, apparently, was aware of what really had taken place. A figure moving so rapidly that it was nothing but a flash of light had been seen to streak toward the falling engine and send it hurtling into the channel. That was all. No one had the slightest idea who the figure was, where it had come from, or where it had gone.

Red Slade and the workman were visibly shaken by the experience they had just gone through.

"Never seen nothin' like it," the foreman blurted. "There was that engine comin' straight down on us. Then somethin' shot by overhead and—and we was safe!"

"You sure was lucky, Red," someone yelled.

"Lucky?" Red surveyed the crowd of men gathered around, and there was an odd gleam in his eyes. "Lucky? Who says so? What *was* that thing that shot by me? Sure, sure, it saved our lives—but what *was* it? It was a ghost, that's what it was! This shipyard is haunted!"

"Now hold on, Red——" John Lowell protested.

"No, you hold on!" the yard foreman snapped back. "I'm sorry, Mr. Lowell, but I've had enough. I've worked here fourteen years, but I can't take no more o' this! Skeleton Ships appearin' in the night, ghosts walkin' along the pier in the fog, and now this! I'm through, Mr. Lowell —through!"

"Wait a minute, Red!" Lowell grabbed him by the arm. "You can't do this to me! These men look to you to make their decisions; they follow your lead. If you walk out now they'll walk out with you!"

"I can't help that," Red retorted. "I'm not riskin' my neck in no haunted shipyard for nobody!"

John Lowell was rapidly losing his temper, and it became obvious to Kent that the events of the past few weeks were beginning to tell on the shipyard owner. Red Slade had shaken Lowell's restraining hand free of his arm; Lowell took hold of it again.

"Listen to me, Red—I won't permit this! This is more than just a job. You're not working for me now, you're working for your country. It's more than a matter of loyalty—it's a matter of patriotism!"

Again Slade shook off Lowell's hand.

"I guess I can be just as patriotic in another shipyard as I can here. I said I'm through. And I am!"

Turning his back on Lowell, he walked off. With much muttering, the men began to follow him, first one by one, then in groups. Lowell, watching them straggle off toward the exit gate, said nothing, but there was bitterness in the set of his mouth—bitterness far more expressive than any words he might have spoken.

"It looks," Kent said absently, "as if I've made a mess of things!"

John Lowell looked at him in surprise.

"I don't see what you had to do with it. Just what do you mean, Kent?"

Too late Kent realized he had forgotten himself, almost to the point of revealing that it was he who had been the ghostly apparition. He sought quickly for some plausible explanation.

"Well?" Lowell was looking at him queerly. "What did you mean?"

"Well, just that—that I'm sort of working for you as a private investigator, also as a reporter for the *Daily Planet,* and it—it seems to me I might have solved this mystery long before now. All this could have been avoided if I had."

Lowell's face relaxed. "You're taking your part in this much too seriously. You're not to blame for anything that's happened here, any more than I am. You know," he continued, "I can't blame Red and the others for walking out. What *was* that thing that shot through the air like a thunderbolt and knocked that engine into the channel?"

Kent did not volunteer an answer. Lowell, silent for a moment, said finally: "Kent, I've made up my mind. I know exactly what I'm going to do!"

"What is that?"

"I'm going to call in the FBI! I should have done it long ago!"

Filled with his new resolve, John Lowell wasted no time but hurried off, leaving Kent alone to pursue his investigation.

Nor did Kent waste any time. He went at once to where the broken steel boom lay on the ground. His suspicions were confirmed in a few moments. The boom had been tampered with, the marks clearly showing where someone had sawed partly through the spot where it had jack-knifed, weakening it just enough for the weight of the engine to do the rest.

Having satisfied himself that the near-tragedy had been no accident, Kent moved out to the abandoned pier to investigate the clue he had noticed a short time before. He paused at the spot where the ancient clipper ship lay tied alongside. His eyes sought and found the marks he was looking for—traces of fresh scratches on the deck where, obviously, a gangplank had rested and rubbed.

Who, Kent asked himself, would want to board the old clipper? And why?

An easy bound landed him on the deck, and he proceeded at once to a companionway leading down into the ancient ship's interior. As he descended the stairs, his nerves began to tingle with the same sensation he had had the night before, the feeling that something was about to happen. At the bottom of the stairs a door blocked his path. He turned the handle. It was locked.

"Odd," he said aloud, wondering who could have locked that door—and why. He could easily have forced the door, but decided he had better not; he wanted to leave behind him no signs of his visit. Whatever lay behind that door, he reminded himself, would be of no use to him without the person who put it there. He decided to do nothing now but to board the clipper ship that night under cover of darkness.

He retraced his steps, regained the pier, and

was soon on his way into town, headed for the railroad station. The telegraph office closed at five, he recalled, and it was rapidly getting on toward that hour now. He quickened his pace, not wanting to miss getting a message from White in case one had arrived.

It had, but it was not the sort of message Clark Kent expected. He read it over several times to be sure he did not mistake its meaning. It read as follows:

YOUR STORY GOOD STOP THINGS SEEM TO BE DEVELOPING STOP THIS BEING THE CASE CANNOT TRUST YOU ALONE STOP AM SENDING EXPERIENCED REPORTER TO COVER STORY WITH YOU.

Kent smiled wryly. He could not blame Perry White, yet having another reporter with him would definitely be a nuisance. Well, he would have to accept it gracefully since there was, after all, nothing he could do about it.

He thanked the telegraph operator, stuck the wire in his pocket, and moved toward the door. As he did so, there was a sudden rattle and roar of a train speeding north.

Kent leaned against the door and watched as the long train, packed with men in uniform, rushed past the station and was lost to sight in the distance. He remained standing there looking off up the tracks, long after the train had disappeared. For with the passing of the train, with the sight of the troops gazing out through the windows, he had a sudden forewarning of disaster. He could not say exactly why he had it, could not pin it down. But the feeling was definitely there. And it bothered him.

CHAPTER XII

ENTER LOIS LANE

T HE FOG, a great gray beast, was already
prowling the streets of the town when Kent,
having had his dinner at a waterfront restaurant,
headed for the Lowell Shipyard again. Night,
because of the fog, was shutting in the town
earlier than usual; it would be sufficiently dark
when he took up his vigil aboard the clipper.

He was still vaguely annoyed by the news that
Perry White was sending another reporter to

141

cover the mystery of the Skeleton Ship. He reflected, however, that whoever was sent would not arrive until the following day, and he fully expected the mystery to be cleared up that night.

Why he felt that the night would bring him the solution to the Skeleton Ship riddle he could not exactly say. Probably the feeling sprang from the fact that he had at last uncovered an important clue, something definite with which to plan a course of action. The first thing he would do on reaching the shipyard would be to go aboard the old clipper, conceal himself somewhere on deck, and wait for the person or persons who were carrying on operations behind the locked door he had found that afternoon. Whoever boarded the clipper ship that night would be the culprit he was after. Once captured, Kent had no doubt he could force the guilty one to reveal the explanation of, and the reason for, the Skeleton Ship.

Main Street was empty, for it was the hour when the people of the town sat at their evening meal, bathed in the warm light of the dinner table and sheltered within doors from the cold and creeping fog. The shops bordering the street were closed and dark, the only light being an occasional street lamp that flickered like some giant yellowish candle through the murk. Kent's footsteps echoed on the glistening pavement.

Then, suddenly, he heard the vicious whine of a bullet and a split second later it struck and flattened itself against his temple.

He pretended to stagger and fall sprawling on the sidewalk, where he lay waiting for what might happen next. He did not have to wait long. Across the street stood Barnaby's chandlery shop. A few moments after Kent fell, a beam of yellow light stabbed the darkness of the street as the door of the shop swung open. Two men came out and, peering furtively up and down the street, hurried over to where he lay. They bent over him. One was Barnaby, the other young Tom Gorman.

"We've got to work fast," Barnaby hissed. "Somebody may have heard the shot!"

"Don't be more of a fool than you've been already," Gorman answered. "You used a silencer, didn't you?"

"Yes, but——"

"Never mind talking!" Gorman said. "Come on! Give me a hand with him."

They lifted Kent and carried him into the shop, placing him on the floor. Then, after closing and bolting the door, they stood over him as they talked.

"Well, you've done it, Barnaby!" Gorman said. "I warned you not to. You know I'll have to report this to my superior."

"I reckon you will," said Barnaby. Between cracked eyelids, Kent saw him filling his short blackened pipe. There was a look of unconcern on his face, as if murder were a casual thing with him. Not so Tom Gorman, whose young face was drawn, his forehead creased with worry.

"To my way of thinking it had to be done," Barnaby continued.

"There was to be no killing—I warned you against that!" Gorman said.

"He knew too much," Barnaby drawled. "He'd have ruined your little game before long."

Gorman's lips tightened and Kent, watching him through the slits of his eyes, saw that he was making a great effort to control his anger.

"Whatever you may have thought," Gorman said finally, "you should have left it to me. That's why I was sent here, to take care of matters such as this." His tone changed. "Well, the damage is done now. I've got to leave. I can't waste any more time."

"I'll get rid of the body," Barnaby said.

Gorman, on his way to the door that led to the rear of the shop, stopped.

"You'll do nothing of the sort. Hide it until I get back—nothing more. I'll decide what's to be done then."

Barnaby did not answer, merely stared at Gorman as he puffed slowly on his short, black pipe. Gorman, apparently certain that his command would be obeyed, continued on into the rear of the shop. He returned a few moments later, wearing a trench coat.

"Get the body out of sight quickly," he said to Barnaby, "but don't do anything else until I return."

"What about the troop trains?" Barnaby asked. "Didn't ye want me to——?'

Gorman cut him short. "After the mess you've made here," he snapped, "I can't trust you with anything as important as that."

"How long will you be?" Barnaby questioned.

"I can't say. It depends on what happens at the shipyard."

He opened the door and was gone into the fog and the night.

Hurriedly Barnaby set to work, and it became obvious to Kent at once that he had no intention of obeying Gorman's order. First he locked the door. Then, moving to a pile of rope, he came back to where Kent lay with a long, stout piece which he proceeded to knot about Kent's middle. Having knotted the rope securely, he straightened up and then paused, his eyes narrowing suddenly. He was looking at Kent's face.

Was he discovered, Kent wondered? Had Barnaby caught the gleam of his eyes, perhaps, as he watched the ship chandler from between his lashes? It appeared that way, for Barnaby leaned forward suddenly and peered closely at Kent's face. Then he reached forward and turned Kent's head from side to side, examining his temples, and then Kent realized what was really bothering Barnaby.

The chandler had discovered the absence of a bullet hole in Kent's head!

His face a study in bewilderment, Barnaby went down on one knee beside the prone figure, staring at the spot where there should have been a bullet hole. Struck by a sudden thought, he laid his hand over Kent's heart. Then he rose to his feet and there was a strange look in his eyes as he stared down at the supposedly dead man.

"Alive!" he muttered. "Well I'll be——! Bullet must have creased him!"

He hesitated for an instant and then evidently made up his mind. He moved quickly to one of the many shelves in the store and, watching him, Kent saw him unwind and cut a long length of wire. Returning to where Kent lay, he began at once to bind the reporter's hands and feet.

Knowing that he could break the bonds with ease, Kent almost smiled as he watched the chandler at work. He wondered, though, what action he should take. He was not long in making up his mind. It would be far more profitable, he decided, to do nothing at the moment and be able to watch Barnaby's movements in the future, than to capture the man now. Barnaby and Gorman would be sure to have alibis. As for the attempt upon his life, it would be the word of an unknown reporter and stranger in the town, against two others of whom one was a respected townsman.

His hands and ankles were now completely bound with wire, and Barnaby dragged him across the floor to the rear of the shop. Reaching the small back room where Kent had first seen young Gorman at work, Barnaby returned to the front of the shop. He was back shortly, carrying with some difficulty a small but evidently heavy anchor, which he secured to the wire that bound Kent's ankles.

If there was any doubt in Kent's mind as to Barnaby's intention, it was dispelled when the chandler pulled back a rattan mat that covered part of the floor and exposed a trap door. To the reporter's ears came the sound of water slapping lazily against wooden pilings. He smiled to him-

self as, with much effort, Barnaby dragged him
and the anchor to the edge of the trap door. In
the next instant he felt himself being pushed
over, and as he fell a distance of about eight feet
to the water he heard Barnaby laugh trium-
phantly. Then the water closed over his head
and the anchor pulled him straight to the bottom!

It needed but the slightest flexing of Kent's
muscles to snap the wires that encircled his
hands and ankles. Then, with amazing speed, he
swam under water until he was sure he had
reached the middle of the river. Not until then
did he come to the surface.

Treading water, he went over his plan of action to be sure it was the right course to follow.
He found no flaws. It was best to let Barnaby—
yes, and Gorman too—think he was dead. When
he thought of Gorman he felt a twinge of re-
gret. He liked the young man and was sorry to
find that he was on the side of the enemy.

It was pitch dark now and time for him to put
in an appearance on the old clipper ship. Kick-
ing sharply, he rose from the surface of the dark

waters and, enclosed in fog, headed for the
Lowell Shipyard, flying low. The fog was thick
but it offered him no difficulty, and in a very
short time he was again standing on the edge of
the abandoned pier.

Despite his swift flight, his clothes were very
wet. Water dripped from them onto the pier and
they clung to his body as if glued there. Yet it
was not the wetness of his clothes, he knew, that
assailed him once again with that feeling of
clammy coldness. He stood motionless for a moment trying to feel the mood that swirled, like
the fog, about him. When night shut down over
the pier, when the heavy mists crept in from the
channel, there was something evil, something
malevolent about this pier.

He smiled grimly; whatever was to come, he
was ready for it!

It came quicker than he expected, and the
shock of it was so great that even he—especially
when surprise followed upon surprise that night
—found himself almost at his wits' end.

He had begun to move quietly toward the old
clipper ship, aboard which he intended to keep

his vigil, when a sharp voice said: "Throw up your hands! I've a gun and I know how to use it!"

It was the voice of a woman. Kent turned quickly and saw a girl coming toward him out of the thick blanket of fog. She was wearing a yellow raincoat that revealed a trim, neat figure. Her face was concealed under the brim of a soft felt hat. She stopped a few feet from him.

"You heard me," she said levelly. "Throw up your hands."

A bullet from the small automatic she held in her hand would have had no more effect on Kent than the touch of a fly. Amused, he decided to play the game with her and slowly raised his arms above his head.

"Now," she said briskly, "we'll get to the bottom of a few things. First, who are you and what are you doing here?"

"I might ask the same of you," he countered.

"You might," she replied, "except that I'm doing the questioning and, if you know what's good for you, you'll do the answering."

He smiled despite himself. He liked this girl,

even though she was far from friendly, and her assurance somehow amused him.

"Well," she said, "are you going to answer my questions or not?"

"I might as well," he said. "My name is Clark Kent."

He heard her sudden intake of breath.

"You——" the girl stammered, "Clark Kent!"

It was now his turn to be surprised, for as the girl spoke his name she lifted her head so that he could see her face. Now he recognized her. It was the girl he had first seen in Perry White's office—the girl White had called Lois.

"Then you're the man I came here to replace," she blurted, and then, realizing she had said something that obviously would offend, attempted to go on. "That is—I mean—Mr. White——"

"I know all about it," Kent said, coming to her assistance. "I got Mr. White's telegram late this afternoon. How did you get here so quickly?"

"I flew to Belfast and hired a car. Once Perry White makes up his mind to do a thing he sees to it that no time is wasted."

Superman caught the white-hot shell
in his bare hands. (Page 104)

"Obviously," Kent murmured. "By the way, what is your full name; and, now that you're here, just what do you plan to do?"

"My name is Lois Lane," she said, "and the first thing I want you to know is that I don't intend to get in your way. Mr. White said to tell you there was really very little wrong with your story; all it needed was some pointing up in spots. However, he said he'd feel easier if the paper had an experienced reporter on the job." She paused, searching for words. "I don't want you to misunderstand, but the truth is I—well, I like to work alone. I can always accomplish more that way. So I'd suggest—that is, if you don't mind—that we work separately and then get together on our stories before sending them in."

Mind working alone? He welcomed it! He was more relieved than he could have told her. While talking to her he had envisioned all sorts of complications that might be brought about by having a girl with him. Still, he did not entirely like the idea of her working alone. For instance, it was infinitely more dangerous than she realized to go prowling about this particular pier at night. He knew by this time the caliber of the men he was dealing with, and he was aware that they would have no more qualms about killing Lois Lane than they would about killing anyone else.

Then there was the Skeleton Ship. The Skeleton Ship with its crew leering down from the rail was a sight to set the strongest nerves quivering. A brief glimpse of it might be enough to send this girl into hysterics. Also there was Captain Joshua Murdock—a skeleton clothed in the tattered and moldy remnants of clothes more than a century old—who prowled the pier at night and who no doubt would make his appearance before dawn.

No, he decidedly did not like the idea of Lois Lane investigating matters in the shipyard on her own. On the other hand, he had a job to do —a job that had become much more than something merely personal. It was linked now with America's great war effort, and he knew that when he was finished, when the case was at last solved, he would find that the Skeleton Ship had much to do with the sinking of those tankers off the coast. But he had to be free to make use of his amazing powers and abilities as the occasion demanded. He could not play watchdog to a girl reporter.

Lois Lane would have to take her chances.

"I don't mind working alone at all," he said. "In fact, I'd prefer it. As you say, we can get together on our stories before sending them back to the paper. Now then, where do we go from here?"

"I'm not going anywhere," she answered. "In your story you said the Skeleton Ship appeared off the end of this pier. I came out tonight to catch a look at it if it appeared again, so I'm staying right here."

"All right," he said. "I've got a couple of things I want to look into back in the shipyard, so I'll leave you here. Pick you up later."

"By the way——!" She stopped him as he turned to go.

"Yes?"

"How did you get out to the end of this pier in the first place? I've been here for more than an hour and I'm sure you didn't pass me. I only heard you when you were coming back."

"That's a funny thing," he said. "I've been wondering about that myself. I guess we didn't see each other because of the fog."

"I thought of that too," Lois said, "only it doesn't seem possible."

"Well," Kent retorted, "I can't think of any other answer that would seem possible." He looked back over his shoulder as he turned to go. "See you later," he called.

Yes, he would see her later, but he had no idea of the circumstances that would surround their next meeting. Had he had the vaguest notion of what was to happen in the next hour, he would certainly have remained with her.

CHAPTER XIII

RETURN OF THE SKELETON SHIP

K ENT WAS WELL hidden from Lois, shrouded
in the fog, by the time he reached the side
of the old clipper ship. He was aboard in an instant, and made his way to a large pile of canvas
which he had noticed on deck that afternoon. He
crouched behind the pile, and from this vantage
point was able to keep an eye on the companionway leading to the locked door below deck.

159

Half hidden, listening to the regular moan of the foghorn in the channel, he let his mind run over the events of the day. So far as he could remember, it had been the most exciting day of his life. If the life of a reporter was as thrilling as this all the time, he told himself, then he certainly hoped Perry White would consider him able enough to give him a permanent job.

Suddenly he remembered what Barnaby had said about the troop trains, and he was vaguely troubled. When young Gorman had cautioned Barnaby to remain at the chandlery shop until he returned, Barnaby had protested that he was supposed to do "something" in connection with the troop trains. Gorman had answered that he would take care of it, that Barnaby could no longer be trusted. Every time Kent had seen those troop trains passing through the station, he had felt an uneasiness, an unfathomable concern stirring within him. He wished now that he knew more about those trains and their destination. Obviously men were being moved to some port to be convoyed abroad. But what port? And when was the convoy due to start overseas? And what——? His mind could not frame the seemingly innumerable questions that chased each other through his brain. He knew only that within him was a deep and gnawing fear that something might happen to those boys—something which he must prevent if he could.

Suddenly he heard a sound that was foreign to the fog-bound night. It came sudden and sharp, and in an instant he had forgotten the past and was alive only to the present, poised and waiting for what was now to come. Someone was coming aboard. As he watched, he saw a dark shape moving against the gray curtain of the fog. It came from the pier, crossed a plank laid from pier to ship, and landed with a muffled thud on the deck. It did not seem like anything human at all. It could only be described as a mass of hunched blackness; and as it slipped silently across the deck to the companionway, Kent felt a slight shudder pass through him. It was not a shudder of fear but an instinctive recoiling against an evil and unknown thing.

As the shape vanished down the well of the companionway, Kent began to strip off the disguise he wore as a mild-mannered reporter. This, he thought, might well turn out to be a job for Superman and he intended to be ready for it. It was as Superman then, magnificent in blue tights and red cape, that he, too, crossed the deck of the companionway. He paused at the head of the stairs and looked down. The door at the bottom of the stair well was closed, but a bar of light showing beneath the door indicated someone was within. Superman descended the steps.

Reaching the bottom, he paused before the door and listened. Inside the room someone was moving about. He heard a chair scrape across the floor, then the sound of several mysterious "clicks," as if switches of some kind were being snapped on or off. Then came the one sound that made everything clear to him—the high whine of a short-wave radio sender. Someone in that room was sending a message in code!

His first thought was to burst into the room. His hand was already on the knob when he realized the message was undoubtedly going to an enemy submarine somewhere offshore. He turned swiftly, leaped up the stairs and regained the deck. In a moment he was off into the night, red cloak streaming, traveling with the speed of a bullet.

What followed happened in the space of minutes.

His ear attuned to the oscillator beam of the short-wave sender, he followed it straight as an arrow across the channel and out over the rolling ocean, his X-ray eyes piercing the blanket of fog in search of the enemy sub. Suddenly he lost the beam. He banked with the speed and precision of a pursuit plane, circling to pick it up again. Then, as an electric whine in a higher pitch fell upon his ears, he realized that the clipper ship had stopped sending and that now he was picking up the answering message.

Nothing suited him better! The beam of the answering oscillator guided him straight and true, and soon a long whale-like shape in the distance told him the enemy sub lay dead ahead.

He hung, poised over the water, gathering his energies for the task ahead of him. About him crackled the electric dots and dashes of the answering oscillator. Ahead of him lay the sub. A grim smile creased his lips as, wrapping his scarlet cape about him, he dove down.

He pierced the murky waters with scarcely a ripple, and his eyes sought and found the long gray steel shape below the water-line. Then, with the speed and precision of a well-aimed torpedo, he shot forward, gathering momentum as he moved.

Sweeping under the sub, following her length till he reached the stern, he forced his shoulders between the twin propellers and began to push, sending the underseas craft through the water at a staggering speed. From within, and from the open conning tower above, came hoarse and muffled shouts. He laughed heartily to himself, picturing the amazed faces of the crew.

It is certain that the submarine crew never knew what had struck them, but it is certain also that they tried to do something about it. It became obvious to them in a short time that they were being driven toward the shore and captivity. Although they had no idea what force was driving them, they attempted to counteract it by

*Superman forced his shoulders between
the twin propellers.* (Page 164)

immediately reversing the engines at full speed.

The effort was doomed to failure. As the twin screws spun into action, with Superman wedged between them, each blade was sheared off as it struck his body. The submarine and her crew were now completely at his mercy and it was but a brief time before he arrived with his cargo in front of the Coast Guard Station.

He had no need to wait to see what the outcome would be. At the first sight of the approaching sub, a siren began to wail a warning. Great lights glared out across the water, playing up and down the long gray enemy craft. As he left the scene, dashing back to where another job still awaited him aboard the old clipper, he saw a cutter bearing an armed crew cleaving the water toward the helpless sub. There was no doubt in his mind that the men would be captured. He laughed aloud as he reflected that although they might answer many a question put to them by the authorities, they would never be able to answer the question of how they got to the Coast Guard Station!

Scarcely five minutes had passed when his feet

again touched the deck of the old clipper. Reaching the companionway, he looked down into the well of darkness and was relieved to see the bar of light still showing beneath the door. His bird had not yet flown. In fact, it became evident to him almost at once that the person inside the room was still trying to get in touch with the sub whose message had been interrupted, for he could hear the oscillator key and there was an urgent note in its whine.

He turned the knob, threw open the door, and confronted—the Old Man!

He was seated before an elaborate short-wave sending and receiving set. He turned sharply on hearing Superman enter, his hand still resting on the sending key. With a muttered oath, he leapt to his feet, the movement sending the chair crashing to the floor.

It must have appeared to him as if a creature from Mars had burst in upon him, for his eyes, peering out from under their heavy gray brows, looked him up and down in stark wonderment. The Man of Steel stood before him for the first time, arms akimbo, red cape flaring out behind him—and his brain could not believe what his eyes beheld.

His voice when it came from his throat rasped with fear and disbelief.

"Who—or what—are you?" he choked.

"That doesn't matter much, my friend," said Superman.

The Old Man had fallen back against the short-wave apparatus, his hands gripping it for support. Beads of sweat stood out on his forehead, and his eyes shone with fear. But as Superman stepped toward him, an automatic appeared as if by magic in the hand of the Old Man.

"Keep your distance," he quavered. "Take another step and I'll shoot!"

Superman smiled, then broke into a chuckle. The Old Man might be holding a pea-shooter for all the good the automatic would do him.

Superman took another step forward.

The Old Man, backing away from the oncoming figure in the scarlet cape, pulled the trigger.

The tiny cabin echoed and re-echoed with the

thunder of the shots as bullet after bullet bounced off Superman's chest. As the Man of Steel reached his antagonist, the Old Man was still pressing the trigger spasmodically, even though there was no sound now but the click of the hammer on empty cartridges. Ripping the gun from the Old Man's hand, Superman forced him back into an open locker and turned the key.

Superman now began to examine the cabin minutely. A swift glance over the short-wave sending and receiving set told him it was a powerful one, capable of sending a signal many hundreds of miles. In the drawers of a near-by desk he found charts of the coastline, geodetic maps of that section of the country, pictures and designs of coastwise vessels. There were graphs showing the tonnage of vessels and giving dates of embarkation. Against some of these were check marks which Superman soon came to understand meant that those particular ships had been sunk.

His eye suddenly lit on the name of the *Carinthia*. Her tonnage as well as her speed were indicated. Against her name, written in ink, were the words: "Possible Troopship—clears from Maidenhead." He thumbed feverishly through the remainder of the list and came across six names of ships with similar legends written beside them. The graphs clutched tightly in his hand, he stood a moment motionless, his mind's eye seeing in retrospect those troop trains passing through the station on their way north. He saw too that although he had sunk one sub and brought another into port there were many others lurking in the depthless ocean, waiting to strike——.

Suddenly a scream pierced the darkness and the fog and found its way into the cabin. It was a woman's scream, shrill and unearthly as only a woman can scream, and he knew at once that Lois Lane was in trouble!

In a fraction of a second he was on deck. Another fraction had barely passed before he reached the pier and was running forward.

Then suddenly he stopped, caught up short despite himself by a second sight of the dreadful thing. At the end of the pier, rising and falling eerily with the tide, was the Skeleton Ship, her

rail lined with a grisly crew. On the pier itself—
his fleshless jaws agape with ghostly mirth—was
Captain Joshua Murdock. And held fast in his
arms, struggling frantically to free herself, was
Lois Lane.

CHAPTER XIV
THE UNMASKING

CHILL AND numbing fear would, at that moment, have shattered the reason of a lesser man. It was a devil's brew of a night, and the "Powers of Evil" were abroad in legion, screaming through space, dancing on the whirling fog, laughing wildly at the satanic scene that met the eyes of Superman. Grotesque and goggle-eyed faces glowed at him through the mists, voices moaned and shrieked, and glue-like

172

fingers clutched at his legs as he strode forward. These things did not exist, but he could almost believe they did, such was the sense of the supernatural that overwhelmed him! One stride was enough to bring him within reach of Captain Murdock. The captain of the skeleton crew saw him coming and flung Lois from him, sending her spinning to the edge of the pier where she collapsed. And now, free to defend himself, he awaited the Man of Steel, his death's-head grinning evilly through the fog, his crew leering down from the deck of the ghost-ship behind him.

Speed and power were behind the fist that landed on the skeleton's jaw, and Captain Murdock dropped limply in his tracks. As his fist landed against the other's face, Superman knew at once that he was dealing with nothing supernatural.

Captain Joshua Murdock was made of flesh and blood.

Yet, staring up at him from the pier was a skeleton face that glowed phosphorescently through the murk.

Phosphorescence—that was it! Superman reached down and in an instant had snatched the mask from the man's face, a mask that bore the picture of a death's-head done in luminous paint! No skeleton, no Captain Murdock, lay upon the pier now. The prostrate figure was that of an ordinary man.

And the man was Red Slade!

It cannot be said of Superman that he was shocked, but if ever he came close to being shocked it was at that moment. Red Slade was John Lowell's foreman, the man whose life he had saved that afternoon, the one person he would never have expected to find beneath the skeleton mask of Captain Murdock. What did it mean? What connection had the foreman of Lowell's shipyard with the web of espionage that was being woven out there across many miles of the broad Atlantic? Even as these questions danced through his brain the answers presented themselves and he knew, beyond all possibility of doubt, that Red Slade was a foreign agent. The Yankee twang which colored the man's voice, the rugged simplicity of his manner, all these meant nothing. Red Slade was the instrument of evil, the diabolical power responsible for the sinking of many ships, the loss of many American lives. Much as his reason fought against it, much as his brain revolted against the shock, Superman knew it could not be otherwise.

Oddly enough, he felt at this same moment a certain vague pity for John Lowell. It was more than unfortunate that a man to whom the future of America meant so much, to whom the completion of the one hundred PT-Torpedo Boats on schedule was so vital, should be tricked so easily and so wantonly by an enemy agent. As he thought this, Superman determined that John Lowell would not be disappointed, that he would definitely see his contracts fulfilled on time.

Slade moaned and began to stir. Superman smiled as he saw this, realizing in himself a new power—the power of restraint. One blow of his mighty fist, its force unchecked, would easily have killed the man. Superman had consciously curbed the strength that surged through his arm as he had struck the blow. He was glad to see that the man was now regaining consciousness, and in a short time as well.

There were a hundred questions he wanted to ask Slade, and he waited with impatience as the man slowly regained his senses. His impatience became the more acute when he remembered the Old Man locked in the cabin of the clipper ship and realized that even now he might be trying to make his escape. From the corner of his eye he saw too that Lois was beginning to move and realized that she was a little too close to the edge of the pier for safety. His senses tuned to any movement aboard the clipper ship and any dangerously sudden consciousness on the part of Lois, he stood over Red Slade waiting for the man to open his eyes. Slade's lids fluttered and he stared up through the fog at the red-cloaked figure above him. Fear crept into his eyes; yet as Superman met and held them with the power of his own he saw their craftiness as well.

"Get up!" he ordered.

Slade got to his feet. He presented an odd figure garbed in the clothes of a past century and

divested of the luminous "skeleton-mask."
There was something incongruous, even foolish,
about the man now that the death's-head disguise had been removed, especially as he stood
against the background of the Skeleton Ship itself. The vessel—her broken spars standing gaunt
and stark in the fog, her crew leering insanely
from her rail—was still anchored at the end of
the pier, and that was what made Red Slade
seem foolish. He was now an ordinary man
against the background of the supernatural.

"Well, Slade," said Superman, "I'm afraid
your little game is finished. I've a lot of questions
to ask you, and if you know what's good for you
you'll be quick with the answers."

Slade regarded him with shifty eyes. Although
he knew he was in the presence of a superior being, his nerves were strong enough to make him
try to brazen the thing through.

"I don't know who you are," he said, "and I
don't much care. Just one thing, Mister—you
ain't gettin' nothin' outa me."

Superman smiled, for he knew how easy it
would be to change the other's mind. He won-

dered how far he would have to go before Slade
gave him the information he wanted. He de-
tested pain of any sort and would have spared
the man before him, yet he was determined to
clear up the mystery of the Skeleton Ship as
quickly as possible. He had more than one
reason for this. His chance for a reporter's job
on the *Daily Planet* depended a great deal on
the speed with which he secured his story, but
beyond this was something far more important
—the knowledge that the lives of many men were
at stake and that materials of war might go to
the bottom of the Atlantic if he did not work
fast.

"Slade," he said, "let's get a few things
straight. You will answer my questions whether
you want to or not. Either you'll answer them
willingly or I'll have to use force."

Slade did not mistake his meaning; the foreman clearly understood what was in store for
him if he did not answer. Despite this, all he said
was, "Well, I told you once I ain't got nothin'
say."

Superman disliked using the tactics of a bully
but he saw no other way. He grabbed the man's

*Speed and power were behind the fist that landed
on the skeleton's jaw.* (Page 173)

wrist, his fingers tightening with a grip of steel. Sweat broke out on Slade's forehead and a moan escaped his lips.

"Now answer me: What is the meaning of the Skeleton Ship? What is the trick behind it?"

Slade gasped in agony, sweat running in little rivulets from his forehead. His lips were blue with pain, but he kept them tightly closed, refusing to voice the answer Superman must know.

"Answer me!" Superman fought against the sympathy that welled up within him even for an enemy; he knew that the agony of his clutching grasp would force the man to answer in the end, and he desperately wished to save him from further pain.

Slade's voice was so weak it could hardly be heard, as he faltered: "I ain't—sayin'—nothin'!"

There were the tankers, there were the hundreds of lives lost and those that might be lost, there were the troop trains moving north. This man must speak, Superman resolved, must tell him what he needed to know for the complete solution of the mystery. He was forced again to tighten his grip.

It was at that moment that Lois Lane, who all this time had been stirring fitfully, regained full consciousness. From the corner of his eye Superman saw her as she struggled to her feet and looked wildly about her. One glance was enough; he knew immediately that the horror of what she had undergone only a few moments before still lingered with her. Even as he attempted to force an answer from Slade, he saw a shudder go through the girl as she suddenly caught sight of the specter-ship that loomed above them through the fog. For a moment she again seemed on the verge of collapse. Then in an instant the fear that might have made her run away became an overpowering desire to come to grips with the thing that threatened. Something like a sob and a shriek came from her lips, and with arms upraised she ran at the Skeleton Ship— ran at it and through it, it seemed to Superman, and vanished from his sight. The sound of a splash told him that she had fallen from the pier into the treacherous waters of the channel.

He released Slade, who fell at his feet. In a fraction of a second he was in the water, his powerful arms cleaving a path to where Lois was struggling frantically. When she was safely in his grasp he turned again for the pier. In her fear Lois fought him, beating her small fists against his chest, striving to escape from his arms. Superman handled her delicately, aware that his powerful hands and arms might easily bruise her. Because of this it took him several minutes to get her back to the pier, holding her gently and swimming with long easy strokes against the current.

Regaining the pier he put her down carefully and, having assured himself that she was in no danger, returned to the spot where he had left Red Slade. But Slade was gone! Not only that, but the Skeleton Ship had disappeared as well! It was as if it had never been there at all. There was nothing now but the smothering fog, the empty pier, and the eerie moan of the foghorn off in the channel.

Even as he thought this Superman was aware that the clue to the entire mystery lay close at hand. Things were not the same. Aside from his unmasking of Red Slade, there was something else—something he had learned only in the last few minutes. Try as he might he could not determine what it was. It annoyed him. It was something vital, he knew. Why could he not recall what it was? He *must* remember—it was important. He reviewed the events that had just taken place. He had seen Lois rush toward and apparently run through the Skeleton Ship and fall into the water; he had released Red Slade and gone to her rescue. Not wishing to frighten her further he had wasted minutes handling her gently and had swum back to the pier instead of flying. During those few minutes something had happened that he was now trying to remember. Had he seen something? Had he felt something? He could not recall.

He was undecided now whether to go in search of Red Slade or to return to the cabin of the clipper ship and continue the questioning of the Old Man which had been interrupted by Lois' scream. Slade, he knew, could not get far without being apprehended and he decided the best course of action would be to return to the cabin. He must first see to Lois, however, who was stirring fitfully where she lay on the pier. It was a matter of a few moments for him to return to the clipper ship, put on his ordinary clothes which he had left behind the pile of canvas on deck, and return to the pier. As Clark Kent, bespectacled and mild-mannered, he approached Lois, who was now sitting up, looking about her in a bewildered fashion.

"You!" she exclaimed. "Where have you been? So many things have happened to me!"

She recounted the story he knew so well—her first sight of the Skeleton Ship, the approach of Captain Murdock, her struggle with him, and all that followed. He listened patiently, anxious to get this over with that he might return to the clipper ship.

As Lois finished the account of how she had been brought safely to the pier in the arms of some strange being, she fixed Kent with a look that had in it something of disdain.

"And where were *you* during all this?" she inquired.

He understood the meaning of her tone at once. He had deliberately fashioned the disguise of Clark Kent to trick others into believing him mild-mannered and lacking in courage. During his first meeting with Lois he had been aware of her appraising eyes, and he knew that she did not consider him worthy of admiration. The tone of her voice now, however, implied more than a lack of respect; it carried with it a definite note of pity.

"I was up at the other end of the shipyard," he said, "following up several clues. I'm afraid they didn't lead to much."

She smiled. There was pity in the smile too, and he was aware of what she was thinking. In her eyes he was not only a rather spineless young man of little consequence, but a callow and inexperienced reporter as well. While he had been off investigating several tame and inconsequential clues which had come to nothing, she had been living through an experience which she would not soon forget and which supplied her with a good deal of colorful material to be woven into a story for the *Daily Planet*. So far as Lois Lane was concerned Clark Kent could hardly be expected to make the grade as a newspaper reporter.

He smiled inwardly as he said, "I don't think there's much more we can accomplish here tonight. I suggest we go on into town. Where are you staying?"

She mentioned the name of a small hotel on Main Street, and agreed that there was little more that they could do. He walked with her to the gate of the shipyard and then left her to find her own way to her hotel, explaining that he would be going on toward his. He waited only long enough for the fog to hide him from her, and then, disdaining the gate, leaped over the barbed-wire fence of the shipyard and again made his way to the old clipper ship.

He walked to the companionway and was about to descend the stairs to the cabin below when he stopped. Voices were raised in argument. He paused, listening. One was the voice of the Old Man, the other a voice familiar to him which he could not quite place. He listened intently. The Old Man was saying: "You haven't a chance, I tell you. If you try——"

The other answered: "Don't be a fool. I've got a gun and you haven't. Do as I say or—— All right, you're asking for it!"

A shot rang out through the fog, followed by another and still another! Even as he heard the Old Man cry out Clark Kent was leaping down the stairs.

This had been a night of surprises, but now he witnessed the biggest surprise of all as he burst into the cabin. On the floor, holding his side, and apparently breathing his last, was the Old Man. Standing in the center of the cabin, a smoking gun in his hand, was John Lowell!

CHAPTER XV

SPECIAL INVESTIGATOR

LOWELL'S FACE reflected a mixture of fear and annoyance on seeing Kent.

"Kent!" he exclaimed. "Where did you come from?"

Kent's gaze shifted from the Old Man on the floor to Lowell.

"How did this happen?" he questioned.

Lowell's lips set in sudden grimness.

"The dirty spy!" he snapped. "I've been watching him and this cabin for the last two weeks. I didn't want to do anything until I could catch him red-handed. Well, I did tonight. I came in here and found him sending a message on the short-wave apparatus. He pulled a gun on me and fired. He missed, thank heaven—but I didn't. I got him on the first shot."

Kent understood what must have happened. When Lois screamed, he had rushed from the cabin to help her, leaving the Old Man in the locker. He had fully expected to return, but matters had occupied him longer than he expected. The Old Man somehow had broken out of the locker and started to send another message to the enemy. Then Lowell had come upon him.

It all added up very nicely, all, that is, save one thing: why hadn't Lowell told him about his suspicions concerning the Old Man? Why had he been so secretive? As these questions flashed through his mind, they were followed by yet another: what was it he had seen while swimming back to the dock with Lois? He had noticed *something*, yet could not remember what it was.

And he had the feeling that it was something vital.

Lowell was speaking.

"We've got to get our spy friend here to a doctor. One of us ought to stay here, though, in case any answering messages start coming through. Do you know how to reach Dr. Carroll's office?"

"No," said Kent.

"He's on Wharf Place just off High Street. You can't miss it. Suppose you take this man up there, while I stay here and wait for anything that may come through?"

Lowell wanted to get rid of him. Kent was as sure of that, quite suddenly, as he was of being Superman. But what was Lowell's motive? Was he in league with the enemy? Impossible, since he had just risked his life to capture the Old Man. Had he merely made a suggestion, after all, without any desire whatever to get rid of Kent? No, for Kent depended completely on his superior perceptions—and he knew they were not wrong this time. Lowell did want to get rid of him. Well, he would pretend to fall in with the other's plans, whatever they might be.

"All right," he said. "I'll take him to the doctor's and get back here as quickly as I can."

"Good," Lowell said. "I'll be waiting for you."

The Old Man had ceased to groan, and lay quietly on the floor, his hand pressed against his side. One look at his ashen face was enough to tell Kent that whatever could be done to save his life must be done quickly.

He gathered the Old Man into his arms, moved toward the door, and turned once more to Lowell.

"I'll be back as soon as I can," he said, and left the cabin.

Once on deck, he took to the air, and flew with his burden to the house of the doctor. Wharf Place was fortunately deserted, and he alighted gently on the walk. It was a matter of moments to find the doctor's house. He rang the bell urgently.

The door was opened by a short, compact man with a sharp face surmounted by a thatch of pure white hair. Gray eyes peered intently at Kent from behind rimless spectacles.

"Yes?"

"Are you Doctor Carroll?"

"Yes. Come in."

The doctor had sized up the situation at once. Without another word, he led Kent into his office, where he helped him deposit the Old Man on an operating table.

"This man's been shot," Kent said. "He needs attention badly."

"Help me get his clothes off," said the doctor. "No, don't bother to unbutton his shirt. Rip it."

As they worked over him, the Old Man groaned and opened his eyes. He struggled to rise and gently they prevented him. Then, for the first time, he saw Kent.

"Kent," he murmured weakly. "Where— where'd you—come from?"

"Don't talk," said Kent. "Just take it easy."

"No! No!" Again he tried to struggle up from the table. A spasm of pain shot across his face and he fell back. "Lowell," he gasped. "Where's Lowell?"

"Never mind that now," said Kent.

"Got to. It's—important. The convoy——" He

paused to get his breath, his chest heaving. It was then that Kent noticed a strange thing. The Old Man's face was seamed and lined with the marks of age, his hair matted and gray. His chest, on the other hand, was bronzed and muscular and the hair there was black.

Even Kent was startled. He looked at the Old Man's face closely, making use of the keen vision of Superman. And, for the first time, he saw that the Old Man was not old at all. The matted gray hair was a wig, the eyebrows false, the lines and creases in the face clever make-up.

"Doctor—wait!"

Kent leaned forward and removed the wig from the Old Man's head. The doctor gasped. Kent went on, removing the heavy gray eyebrows and, with a towel, the grease paint from the face. The Old Man did not try to stop him, but lay unprotesting on the table, breathing painfully. And when every bit of make-up had been removed, it was indeed a young man who lay on the table—a young man Kent knew very well.

"Sorry I fooled you like this, Kent," he said, smiling painfully.

The doctor interposed.

"I don't know what's going on here," he said, sharply, "but one thing I do know. I've got to get to work on this man quickly."

"Wait a minute!"

It was the young man who spoke.

"Kent," he went on, "listen to me. I know how things look. You think I'm an enemy agent. Well, I'm not. Get—get my wallet out of—my coat." Kent did so. "There's a false back to that wallet—a flap you can lift up. See it?" Kent did. "Look at those papers."

Kent examined the papers carefully. The doctor did not wait for him to finish, but began his examination of the bullet wound.

"So that's it," Kent said finally. "Special Investigator, eh?"

"That's right," said the young man between gritted teeth.

"Then what about Lowell?"

"That's what I've been trying to tell you—that's what's so urgent!" He pushed the doctor from him. "Listen, and get this straight, because I've got to depend on you. Three hours ago the biggest troop convoy we've sent across the Atlantic cleared from Maidenhead. Four troop-ships, six destroyers."

"But you——" Kent began, then stopped.

"Yes? Go on," the young man said.

"You yourself were sending information to a submarine when I first found you in the cabin of the clipper ship!"

"The information I was sending about the convoy was false. I was giving them a wrong steer. Lowell's your man. No, don't ask questions—there's no time for that. Right now, if I don't miss my guess, Lowell's back in that cabin working the short-wave for all he's worth. There's a flotilla of enemy subs out there, and by this time they've probably gotten the location of that convoy. But there may still be a chance. You've got to get to Lowell and stop him if it's not too late already!"

It was a long speech for the wounded man, gasped out rather than spoken, and now he sank back on the table, his chest heaving painfully.

Kent knew the man on the table spoke the truth. He was a Special Investigator—his papers proved that. Disguised as an old man, he had uncovered the short-wave apparatus and had used it to send the sub flotilla in the wrong direction. But now, at this very moment, Lowell was setting them right. For all he knew, during these very seconds the enemy submarines might be firing torpedo after torpedo into those troopships!

He knew what he had to do, his course of action was clear. He turned to go.

"I'll do what I can," he said. "By the way, your name *is* Tom Gorman, isn't it?"

The young man smiled through the pain he was undergoing.

"Sure thing," he said. And he added, "You've got a lot of questions to ask me, and I'll be glad to answer 'em, if I pull through. But that convoy's the important thing now. So get going!"

There was truth in Tom Gorman's eyes as they met those of Clark Kent—truth and strength and an unwavering faith.

Without a word, Kent departed.

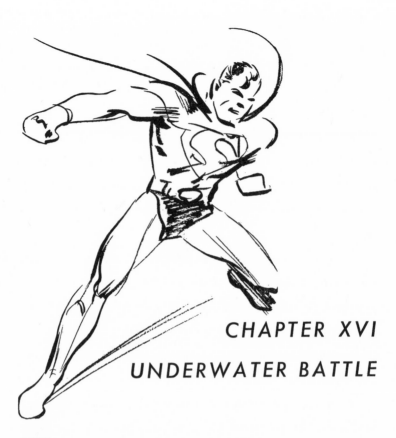

CHAPTER XVI

UNDERWATER BATTLE

THIS WAS A job for Superman!

Standing outside Dr. Carroll's house in the fog-bound street, Kent was certain of this. Somewhere out on the broad Atlantic steamed a convoy carrying thousands of American soldiers. Lying in wait for that convoy, like sharks lurking in the ocean's depths waiting for the kill, was a flotilla of enemy submarines, prepared to send those ships to the bottom. Needed here as

198

never before were the strength, the skill, all the miraculous powers of Superman!

A glance up and down the street assured him he was not observed. He stripped off his everyday disguise of Clark Kent. Then, red cape streaming in the wind, he leapt lightly into the air, heading straight for the old clipper ship.

He landed gently on the deck and, drawing his cape about him, was down the steps of the companionway and into the cabin.

John Lowell turned from the short-wave apparatus as Superman entered. Superman strode to where he sat, sent him spinning from his chair with one mighty blow, and with another smashed the short-wave set into a thousand pieces. Even as he did so, he heard the sound of shots and felt bullets striking his back. He turned to confront Lowell who, from the floor, was emptying a pistol at him. He could not waste time. He could divine, from the look on Lowell's face, that he was too late—that the submarines even now were making their way at full speed for the doomed convoy. He lifted Lowell from the floor with his left hand.

"You murderous traitor!"

His fist snapped up against the shipyard owner's jaw, and this time he did not pull his punch. Lowell slumped to the floor without a word, without a sound.

Lowell disposed of, Superman regained the deck of the old clipper and, spreading his red cape, hurtled into the air and out over the rolling Atlantic. Never had he flown so fast, never had his eyes peered more keenly in search of something, never before had he so gathered his strength for a job that must be done—a job only Superman could do!

Coursing out across the sky, he saw below him the broad expanse of the ocean. Through the night and the fog his eyes searched for the black shapes of the convoy, searched anxiously, almost fearfully. He saw nothing, nothing but the black and frightening water below him.

On he sped, red cape spread to the wind, a hawk in flight, sharp eyes peering, ever searching.

He must not be too late. Thousands upon thousands of lives depended on him. Yet he felt desperately that he was too late, that already the subs had got in their deadly blows, that the convoy even now lay at the bottom of the heaving surface below him. Again, for some unaccountable reason, the question that had been bothering him all this time, that had lain at the back of his mind, came to the fore: What was it he had seen while swimming back to the pier with Lois? It seemed ridiculous to think of anything so inconsequential at a time like this, yet it annoyed him, and perhaps it was not so inconsequential as it seemed.

Then he saw the convoy!

He counted the ships with an anxious heart. There were ten—and he breathed easier. He made out the heavy, squat outlines of the troopships, and the streamlined shapes of the six destroyers. They were running without lights, and he saw them only as blacker shapes against the black of the ocean. He increased his speed.

He reached the convoy and hovered over it protectingly. On the bridge of each ship below him he saw figures standing silent and tense, and he was aware that the men aboard had no idea

Then Superman saw the convoy. (Page 201)

when or how the enemy might strike, of what
moment might be the last.

The four huge troopships wallowed along,
one behind the other. The six sleek destroyers
guarded them—two in the lead, one on each side,
and two more bringing up the rear. With no
moon to light the ocean, all ten ships looked like
shadowy phantoms.

They were no more phantoms, however, than
were the underwater craft Superman now
spotted ahead and off to the right. He counted
five of them, five long slim shapes lying just beneath the surface. Three lay on one side of the
convoy, two on the other. And into this trap,
unaware of the danger, the convoy was slowly
steaming.

He had long before decided on what he would
do. There was no need now for thought, only
for action.

He shot forward toward the first sub, diving
underwater not ten yards from her stern. As his
terrific speed carried him past the undersea craft,
he reached out and with his left hand ripped off
her rudder. The force of the action swung the

enemy pigboat around. Now, instead of pointing toward the convoy she pointed away from it, and, rudderless, was unable to bring herself again into position.

The first sub rendered useless, Superman headed for the second, where he performed the same operation. His keen ears picked up a sound somewhat like a combined rumbling and hissing. Looking backward underwater he saw that the first sub, using her only chance for safety, was "blowing" her tanks and coming to the surface.

He smiled grimly, knowing the second would be forced to follow suit, and turned his attention to the third.

Even as he did so, he heard in the distance the sudden warning shriek of sirens and knew that the surfacing submarine had been sighted by the destroyers. As the sirens sounded a shell whined above him and he struck out for the third submarine. Too late, he saw a deadly torpedo leave her mouth and streak through the water on its way toward one of the troopships.

Quicker than light Superman was after it. He

shot past it and waited in its path. The torpedo struck him squarely in the chest, exploding in a titanic detonation that sent tons of water skyward. He plowed through the seething and boiling water, reached sub No. 3, and wrenched her rudder and propeller free!

And now the ocean depths about him became a thunderous nightmare. Hardly had he ripped the rudder from No. 3, when he heard a rumbling above him and, looking upward, saw the keel of a destroyer pass overhead. Then the "cans" began to drop all about—depth charges that exploded with tremendous force! Strong as he was, he was thrown about dizzily as each depth charge detonated. He struggled on against the bubbling, seething water, pitting his strength against the mighty forces that raged about him!

Another destroyer cut the water above him, and again he saw the deadly "cans" plummeting down from the surface. But they were useless here! Sub No. 4 lay a good quarter of a mile ahead of him under the surface. He worked fast. He reached out, grabbed one of the depth charges, and, treading water, hurled it with all his strength toward No. 4. Such was his power, that even with the force of the water against it the "can" almost reached the sub before it exploded.

He repeated this action again and again. Some of the depth charges exploded as he laid hands on them, others as he was in the act of throwing them, but some reached their mark.

A battered and torn No. 4 sank like a dead monster into the black depths of the Atlantic.

He turned his attention now to the fifth submarine—but she was nowhere to be seen, for she had turned tail and fled.

Superman rose to the surface.

Three of the five enemy submarines lay on the water, their crews lining the rails. Cutters loaded with armed U. S. Marines were putting off from the destroyers and making their way toward the enemy craft. In a moment or two the Marines would land, it appeared, and the situation was already well in hand.

Hovering in the air above the scene, his great cloak spread, Superman watched as the submarines' crews were taken off, the guns on the destroyers blew the underwater marauders out of the water forever, and the convoy formed again and steamed eastward.

His eyes followed them out of sight over the horizon and, as he turned for home, he smiled a farewell. Then, suddenly, he began to chuckle. The chuckle became a delighted laugh. The thing he had been trying to remember, the thing gnawing all this time at the back of his brain, had come to him at last. He knew now what it was he had seen while swimming back to the pier with Lois.

And he laughed because with that knowledge came the realization that the mystery of the Skeleton Ship was solved.

CHAPTER XVII

THE MYSTERY SOLVED

"Now just a second. Let me get a few things straight."

The *Daily Planet* re-write man squashed out his cigarette in the ash tray on Perry White's desk, shifted to a more comfortable position, and looked at Kent inquiringly.

"You mean to tell me," he went on, "that that Skeleton Ship was nothing but a moving picture?"

Kent nodded. "That's all," he said.

"By Harry, I don't believe it! I *won't* believe it!"

It was Perry White who spoke, rapping the desk with his fist.

"Kent, you can't tell me that any sane, normal man could possibly be taken in by such a fake!"

"I didn't say anything about a sane, normal man," said Kent.

"What's that? What kind of gibberish are you talking now?"

"It's not gibberish," Kent answered. "It's the truth, Mr. White. Don't you understand? No man could remain sane or normal under the conditions that existed at the Lowell Shipyard. One of the greatest of human failings is a willingness to believe what one is told to believe. John Lowell saw to it that the minds of the men working for him were sufficiently conditioned, before the Captain Murdock business and the Skeleton Ship was sprung on them. That's why the watchman who first saw the so-called apparition went out of his mind. He was expecting it, he was filled with fear of it, and all he needed was a glimpse of it—just a glimpse—to unbalance him."

"How come, if you know so much about it," said the re-write man, "you yourself were taken in by it?"

"I brought the films back with me," said Kent, "and I'll show them to you later. Don't ask me how or where Lowell had them made. He wouldn't say. But one look at them will show you how convincing they were, especially when seen through a veil of fog, and surrounded by the proper atmosphere of a lonely shipyard at midnight, with foghorns in the distance, and all the rest of it."

"I can see what you mean," said the re-write man. "I've got imagination."

"That's what you're paid for," snapped Perry White. "Stop flattering yourself and get the facts."

The re-write man glared and lit another cigarette.

"Now you say these pictures were shown on the sail of a sailboat that lay off in the channel?"

"That's right," said Kent. "I noticed that sailboat moored in mid-channel a number of times, but paid no special attention to it. And then——"

He paused. He had to explain somehow, yet he could not tell them that he had seen the sail-boat anchored *near the pier* while swimming back with Lois that night.

"Yeah, and then—what?" It was the re-write man again.

"Well, it struck me as rather odd that a sailboat should be moored out in the middle of the channel. I decided to investigate, and did. I found the motion-picture projector, the batteries used to run it, and the film—all carefully concealed, of course—on the boat."

"All they did, you see," said Lois, who had remained silent up to now, "was to bring the sailboat close to the pier, and, at the right time, start the projector. And I can tell you, when you saw that picture in the fog——"

"Quiet, Lois!" snapped Perry White. "This is Kent's story. Let him tell it."

"Well," said Kent, "that's about all there is to tell. I suppose you'd call John Lowell a Quisling; he was actually working in the interests of the enemy, while pretending to be a patriotic citizen. Tom Gorman was sent to the shipyard as a Special Investigator because he was a nephew of Lowell's housekeeper, and it was felt he could keep tabs on Lowell through her—which, of course, was just what he did."

"What about this guy Barnaby? Why did he take a shot at you, if he was working with Gorman?"

Kent laughed.

"Barnaby," he said, "was a little too patriotic. He suspected I was an enemy agent, and apparently he needed nothing more than that suspicion to take the law into his own hands."

The re-write man scratched his head. "Well, I guess that covers everything," he said. "No, wait a minute. What about that business in the shipyard when the boom collapsed and those two birds were almost killed by a falling engine? Who was behind that?"

"Lowell," Kent replied. "His yard foreman, Red Slade, knew too much and he decided to get rid of him."

The re-write man scribbled on a sheet of paper. "Then Slade was in cahoots with Lowell," he said.

Kent smiled. "I should say that was pretty obvious since Slade was playing the part of Captain Joshua Murdock, skipper of the Skeleton Ship." He glanced from the re-write man to Perry White. "I think I've explained the whole business."

White leaned forward across the desk and fixed Kent with a quizzical stare.

"You haven't explained, Kent, how you managed to get free of that anchor Barnaby tied to your ankles when he dropped you through the trap door. And you haven't explained how on several occasions you appear to have been in two places at once!"

What was he to say? So long as Superman existed there would always be things that could not be explained away.

"Well," White insisted, "what's the answer?"

"Yes," said the re-write man, "and how about——?"

"Wait a minute!" Kent rose from his chair. "If you don't mind, gentlemen and Miss Lane, I'm—well, I'm pretty tired. I've given you the story you wanted, Mr. White, and I've thoroughly covered the important points. The rest of it you can figure out for yourself. And if you can't, I don't see that it matters much." He paused, looking at White. "All I want to know," he added, "is whether I'm a full-fledged reporter now or not."

White rose from behind his desk. There was a scowl on his face, and his eyes glinted sharply through his rimless glasses.

"You certainly are!" he said. "Consider yourself one of my staff. There's just one thing to remember: I'll hire and fire you a hundred times before we're through. Just don't pay any attention to it. That's me."

They shook hands.

Lois Lane looked dubious.

"I don't know how you've done what you've done," she said. "You don't look the type. But —well—glad to have you with us."

She extended her hand and Kent shook it. As their eyes met for a second, Kent decided that he liked Lois Lane more than he had thought.

The re-write man scowled.

"There are a lot of fine words floating around

this office," he said, "but I'm the guy that's got to slave over a hot typewriter and get this story written. Now look, Kent, there are still a couple of things——"

"Unexplained?" queried Kent. "Well, figure them out for yourself, old man, figure them out for yourself."

DATE DUE

SEP 30 '97			
MAR 2 1 '99 MAR 0 2 '99			
MAY 1 7 2002			
AUG 3 1 2002			
OCT 1 6 2002			
JUN 0 3 2000 NOV 0 7 2008			
DEC 1 7 2008 FEB 1 2 2009			
ILL 3/28/12 ILL# 87861023			
SEP 2 5 2014			
GAYLORD			PRINTED IN U.S.A